COURAGE OF THE STONE

SHADOW

T0306440

ARIZONA

N

GRAND CANYON

Father
Mountain

Demon
Mountain ▲

Mother
Mountain

Little Colorado River

[PHOENIX]

[TUCSON]

Present Day Names

Father Mountain—*San Francisco Peaks*
Mother Mountain—*Elden Mountain*, Flagstaff
Demon Mountain—*Government Mountain*

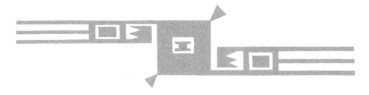

COURAGE OF THE STONE

SHADOW

Helen Hughes Vick

ROBERTS RINEHART PUBLISHERS
Boulder, Colorado

To my sister, Becky Felix, who faced death
with great courage, deep inner strength,
and unwavering faith. She won!

A special thanks to Dr. Connie Stone and Mary Swersey,
archaeologists, for their expertise and support.

Published by
ROBERTS RINEHART PUBLISHERS
6309 Monarch Park Place
Niwot, Colorado 80503
Visit our web site: www.robertsrinehart.com

Distributed to the trade by Publishers Group West

Published in the UK and Ireland by
ROBERTS RINEHART PUBLISHERS
Trinity House, Charleston Road
Dublin 6, Ireland

Copyright © 1998 by Helen Hughes Vick
Cover illustrations copyright © 1998 by Sean Shea

Cover design: Ann W. Douden
Interior design & production: Polly Christensen

International Standard Book Number 1-57098-218-x cloth, 1-57098-195-7 paper

Library of Congress Cataloging-in-Publication Date

Vick, H. H. (Helen Hughes), 1950–
     Shadow   /   by Helen Hughes Vick.
        p.   cm.   —   (Courage of the stone series)
     Summary: In 1180 A.D., Shadow struggles to survive in the
mountains as she tries to rescue her father and her beloved brother,
even though to succeed she must disobey the time-honored traditions
of her Sinagua culture.
     ISBN   1-57098-218-X
     1. Sinagua culture—Juvenile fiction.   2. Sinagua culture—
Fiction,   3. Sex role—Fiction.   4. Survival—Fiction,   I. Title.
II. Series: Vick, H. H. (Helen Hughes), 1950– Courage of the stone
series.
PZ7.V63Sh   1998   98–5248
[Fic]—dc21   CIP
                                                            AC

All rights reserved.

10 9 8 7 6 5 4 3 2 1

Manufactured in the United States of America

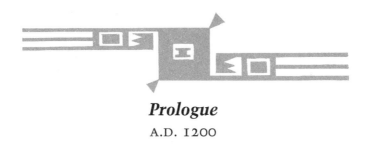

Prologue

A.D. 1200

THE UNEARTHLY WAIL screamed across the starlit night and into Shadow's dream. Terror echoed through Shadow's thirteen-year-old body, setting her heart racing. She curled tighter under her rabbit-skin blanket. Murky images of Sun, her twin brother, invaded her dream: wearing just his loincloth, Sun huddled close to a flickering fire. Another threatening screech shot him to his feet. His hands clutched his spear. Fear consumed his dark face. Shadow's heart raced in rhythm with Sun's heart. She felt his terror. Her skin prickled in alarm, mirroring her brother's fear. Shadow peered through Sun's eyes into the darkness of night, searching as the demon's snarling howls came closer.

Sun sprang in the direction of the sound. The screech wailed from behind him, then to the side of him, surrounding him. Raising his spear, Sun darted into the darkness.

"No!" Shadow screamed, but no sound came out of her mouth. She struggled to follow. Her body turned to stone. "Sun," she broke through her panic. "Do not go, Sun!" Her plea burst from her lips.

She found herself sitting atop her crumpled blanket. The cold, high desert air gnawed at her bare shoulders. Panic consumed her. The sound of her heartbeat thundered in her ears and seemed to fill the small adobe room. Tears washed down her checks. "Sun," she whispered.

Shadow heard Mother mumble in the darkness beside her. A warm hand touched her shoulder. "You are dreaming again, daughter." Mother tugged at Shadow. "Go back to sleep."

Mother breathed in sleep as Shadow snuggled down in the furry blanket. She curled closer to her mother's child-swollen body. Terror, both Sun's and her own, raged within her. The dream hovered in her mind. The demon's screeches rang in her ears. Panic whirled like thick smoke, clogging her throat.

"No, it was not just a dream. It was—it still is, *too real* to be just a dream," Shadow thought. No longer trapped in sleep, her mind clicked in precise thoughts.

This was not the first time she had experienced her twin brother's feelings, even his physical pain. Shadow could not explain it. Perhaps being carried at the same time under their mother's heart had bonded them as one. Sun and Shadow were true to their names. Without each other, there was none.

She knew that somewhere, miles from the safety of their stone village, her brother faced fear and danger. This fear and danger not only threatened Sun's life but her life, also.

Shadow had to defy fear to save Sun and herself, as well.

But how?

$\mathbb{T}$HE GRAYISH LIGHT that comes after night and before sunrise shadowed the world. The A.D. 1200 pueblo village slept against the high desert mountain. Stars faded from the pewter sky. Dreams swirled and danced behind all the villagers' closed eyes.

All, that is, except for a wiery thirteen-year-old girl. The muscles in her oval face pulled tight in concentration. Her dark, almond-shaped eyes squinted against the charcoal shadows. A blanket pieced together from rabbit skins cloaked her bony shoulders and fell down her straight back. Her long, black hair swayed against the blanket's warming folds. A blouse-type covering draped her left shoulder. Her right shoulder lay bare under the blanket. Yucca sandals swung from the woven belt cinching her short leather skirt. Her bare feet climbed the smooth rungs of a log-pole ladder leaning against a wall of the village.

Stepping onto the roof, she stopped and caught her breath. Her knees shook from the fear that was not her own. It was a fear that traveled across miles of forest, cinder-covered hills, and tall mountains that stood between her and her twin brother, Sun.

Shadow scurried to her favorite prayer spot on the flat roof. When the sun's first rays peeked over the horizon, the old village crier would ascend to the roof. His deep voice would awaken the village, announcing a new day. Movement would fill the compacted rooms below. All the log-pole ladders would creak as young and old climbed to the roof to offer their own prayers for the new day.

But now, Shadow had the roof and the world all to herself as Sun's fear swept through her.

Facing the east, Shadow dropped to her knees. She clasped a small eagle feather and closed her eyes. "Please," Shadow whispered over the feather cupped to her lips. "Please, protect Sun. Give him courage. Give me the courage to . . ."

To what?

She, like other females, was forbidden to touch a spear or any other weapon, and she did not even know where Sun was.

Images of evil spirits, monsters, and wild beasts hovered in Shadow's imagination. She tried to push the unreal images out of her mind. Their father, Stone Carrier, was with Sun and would protect him. A new wave of fear washed over her. Whatever danger Sun faced, it was coming closer, and Stone Carrier was unable to stop it.

"Please," Shadow prayed on the feather. "Guide his steps. Strengthen his mind." She recited every prayer she had ever heard, hoping that some guardian spirit was listening so early in the morning. Just to be safe, she must tie the prayer feather to the sacred tree beyond the village's wall. The wind would carry her prayers to any listening spirit. Frustrations halted her prayer. There had to be more that she could do besides just pray.

"Shadow."

Her mother's voice brought Shadow's eyes open. Mother eased her swollen body over the top of the ladder. Her sun-weathered face had the puffy look that forewarned of birth.

New anxiety pricked Shadow's heart. It was apprehension that only women experienced, as only they knew and bore the pain of childbirth. The thought of Shadow's three tiny baby brothers buried side by side burst into her mind. The image of her mother's body lying in the ground near those graves shot panic through Shadow. For many women, childbirth was their last struggle in this life.

"Little sister, it is too early even for prayers." Mother's voice sounded weary. She stood with her hands rubbing the small of her back. Her huge stomach pressed tight against her leather dress.

Shadow leaped up. "I am sorry. I did not mean to wake you."

"You did not." Mother patted her bulging stomach. "This little one did. It wants to escape from its dark cave. Feel." She guided Shadow's hand to feel the bumping mass within her.

2

Shadow smiled at the firm kicking against her hand. "This one feels strong. Not like the others."

"Yes. Girl babies must be heartier." Mother stroked Shadow's hair. "Just as we women must be stronger and more courageous to survive."

Shadow slipped her arms around her mother and squeezed. "A girl. A baby sister." Since her mother's stomach started swelling, she had not let herself even hope for a sister. Among her people, males were prayed for. Each of her tiny brothers who had died had been welcomed with rejoicing and grieved for deeply.

"Maybe there are two sisters waiting to escape," Shadow said, feeling anxious.

"No." Mother's voice was firm. "Your sister is alone under my heart." She touched Shadow's cheek. "Even if there were two babies, no choice would be made between them. I would demand that both babies be allowed to live just as I did with you and Sun."

At Sun's name, Shadow stiffened.

"So, you are up before the birds because you are worried about Sun." Mother hugged Shadow closer. Shadow felt the baby's movement against her own stomach. "I wish that Sun did not need to go with your father to gather obsidian or travel to other villages to trade. Worry chews at my soul every minute they are late in returning. But Sun must learn the ways of his father, of men, just as you are learning the ways of women."

Shadow pulled away from her mother. "I hate being a girl. Becoming a woman is worse: men telling me what I can and cannot do. I despise doing everything that they think is tedious and boring—like grinding corn."

"Men grow the corn."

"But I weed it," Shadow countered. She wondered if Mother knew the frustration that consumed her each time Sun left on a quarrying or trading journey. Because she was a female, she remained behind to haul water, weed, and grind corn while Sun saw and experienced the wonders of the world.

She was as strong as Sun and as smart. Sun had even said so. He had taught her many things that girls were not supposed to do, such as playing ball. She even had her own kicking ball. Sun had smuggled it to her from a trading trip. It came from the tall stone villages in the sweltering desert to the south.

Concealed from the eyes of others, Sun had taught her to kick the leather-covered ball along as she ran. They kicked the ball to each other, running full speed. It was she who made up the game of tossing the ball to each other. The ball was just one of the male activities Sun had taught her. But with each new skill learned, Shadow's frustration mounted. What good were knowledge and skills if she could not use them? If anyone had seen her playing with the ball, village ridicule would have been the least of her punishments. Strict rules of behavior governed the roles of men and women. Each trespass had its penalty.

Mother's gentle voice drew Shadow out of her thoughts. "It is difficult to squeeze into a place that others have carved for you." She brushed her own long dark hair back over her shoulder. "It always has been hard for me."

"You?" Shadow could not believe that being a woman was painful for Mother. Fair Dawn was perfect: loving, quiet, never demanding or quarrelsome. No one ever heard Mother complain about what she did. Everyone loved and sought out Fair Dawn when they were soul-troubled, ill, or injured. Her reputation as a healer put her in high regard.

"But you. . . ." The words would not come as Shadow stared into her mother's penetrating eyes.

Mother cradled her bulging stomach. "Life is not easy for women or for men. Each of us must find a balance between the life we are born into and accepting our self in that place." She spoke with intensity. "Every woman must decide where she will stand, what battles she must fight, and what rules she must break in order to survive within herself."

Realization burst into Shadow's mind. "You refused to kill a female baby born in the shadow of a male baby, as demanded by custom." Shadow watched the pink light brightening the eastern sky, feeling ashamed for not realizing her mother's courage before now.

"Life is too precious to cast off in the name of custom." Mother stepped in back of Shadow and wrapped her arms around her. She whispered into Shadow's ear. "Be patient, little sister. Have faith in yourself. Listen to your heart; it is a very courageous one."

Despite Mother's warm body against Shadow's back, a shiver crawled up it.

2

ONLY SHADOW'S GRINDING, the sound of rock on rock, filled the small room where corn was ground. The other women and girls had finished long ago. Shadow knelt over the well-worn trough-shaped stone. Her knees burned. The small of her back ached as she ground the dried corn in the metate with her hand-held stone. Her fingers, accustomed to the loaf-shaped mano, still cramped with pain at each back and forth movement.

As she worked, Shadow fought the fear surging within her. She did not question why or how she felt Sun's terror. It was just there, as real as the corn being crushed beneath her stone mano. No one would understand what she was feeling. Shadow had never told a living person about experiencing Sun's feelings. The others, even Stone Carrier, thought of her as ill-fated for being born on Sun's heels. They would accuse her of being a witch if she reported the panic lapping within her like water in a puddle as wind blew across it.

Shadow dropped her mano and leaned back on her heels. "This will last Mother four or five days," Shadow thought, satisfied at last. She scooped the last bit of cornmeal out of the metate and poured it into her brown ceramic storage jar. Shadow whipped a thin piece of leather around the jar's narrow opening. She slung the jar to her hip.

Earlier she had hauled enough water and wood to last Mother until she and Sun returned. *Return*—the word thundered through Shadow's mind, and her stomach twisted. Shadow's courage began to crumble like bits of corn as she scrambled out of the grinding room door.

She hurried through a narrow passage between two rows of homes. The mud and rock hallway led into the center of the village. With each step, uncertainty hovered over her shoulder. She had never been more than a day's walk from home and always went with Sun. It would take enormous courage to spend the moonless nights alone. Sleeping on the roof during hot nights were the only times she had ever slept without the safety of walls. Sun or Mother always slept nearby, offering security.

Even finding Sun suddenly seemed impossible. The village men insisted that the outside world was plagued with danger behind every rock and tree. Shadow's legs felt like a toddling baby's. She stopped and leaned against the wall of the passage. It would take more courage than she possessed to venture into the unknown world alone.

"Sun was to be back two days ago," a young voice said. Shadow recognized Spring Breeze's flirting voice coming around the corner of the passage. "Stone Carrier promised that he would bring my father the best black stone before the harvest celebration began."

Winter Dove's squeaky voice responded, "Even if Sun returns tomorrow, there is plenty of time for him to ask you—." Giggling masked the rest of her words.

Shadow pressed her lips together. Jealousy gripped her. Spring Breeze and Winter Dove were her age, thirteen summers. Where their bodies now curved and bumped, Shadow's was as straight as Sun's. They both wore their long hair carefully combed into the puffy, round squash-blossom whirls over each ear that invited the young men to court them. Shadow's hair tangled down her back in the manner of a child. In a few days, Winter Dove and Spring Breeze would dance at the harvest feast. Shadow would herd the younger children and quiet the babies.

"Yes, but only if Sun's *shadow* is not trailing behind him." Spring Breeze's voice rang with dislike. "Shadow is a disgrace to the village. I heard Grandmother whisper that *she* will never be one of *us*. Her own father does not accept her."

Squaring her shoulders, Shadow marched around the corner. Winter Dove and Spring Breeze huddled in front of a low, T-shaped door. Shadow kept her eyes straight, avoiding the girls' stares. They stopped chattering and burst into laughter as she passed by. Shadow's face burned. She longed to yank the whirls of black hair off their silly heads.

"Each woman must decide what battle she must fight." Mother's words echoed in Shadow's mind.

Shadow could not waste precious time quarreling. She had a more important battle to fight—a contest of life or death.

Shadow trekked across the flat, open area in the center of the village, called the plaza. Now that she was leaving the village, it seemed that she was seeing it for the first time. Colors, sounds, smells, and textures never noticed before leaped out at her. She studied the four long rock and mud walls that enclosed the plaza. Each wall contained low T-shaped doorways. A passageway, like the one she had just come through, framed each corner of the plaza. Log-pole ladders leaned against the walls, reaching the second story patios and doorways. Longer ladders stretched to the roof. The brightness of the blue sky burned Shadow's eyes. Smells of dust, burning wood, cooking food, sweaty bodies, and autumn singed her nose. Everything spoke of safety. Shadow slowed her pace.

Babies cried from their cradle boards. Women visited as they wove baskets or rolled cordage from strong yucca fibers. A woman smoothed a deer hide with a stone scraper as her daughter toiled over an antelope hide. Groups of small children chased each other. A near-naked boy collided with Shadow in the middle of the plaza.

The three-year-old peered up at her. "You can be the bear, if you play with us."

With a growl, Shadow lunged at him. "I will eat your toes first, then your nose." The boy escaped, squealing, with three others following. Shadow shifted the storage jug to her other hip. "If only I could just play," she thought.

Shadow scurried past a cluster of women fashioning bowls and mugs from wet clay. She loved the warm, earthy smell of the clay. In a few days, after the clay dried, smoke would curl into the sky as the pottery baked in the firing pit. The potters would hum the firing song to prevent the pots from cracking. Shadow wondered if she would be there to watch the finished wares retrieved from the warm ashes.

Three old men rested with their backs against a sun-drenched wall near Shadow's home. They mumbled in low sounds. Shadow wished she could sit and listen to their stories of courage and the old legends that taught the ways of life.

Shadow's house made up the northwest corner of the plaza. Mother stood beside the door, pressing her hands against her back as she listened to Twisted Hair. Mother nodded as the bitter old woman's complaints salted the air. She smiled when she saw Shadow over the woman's stooped shoulder. "Good, Shadow, you are finished grinding."

Twisted Hair's wails ceased the instant she heard Shadow's name. She whipped around, bumping into her.

"I am sorry," Shadow mumbled. She dodged Twisted Hair and stooped through the low door.

Cool, close air swept over her. The house smelled of old smoke, corn cakes, and the sweet herbs and plants that hung upside down to dry above the cooking area. Pots, mugs, and storage jars, as well as baskets, occupied the area below. Sleeping mats and rolled-up blankets occupied a corner next to mother's medicine containers. Shadow's father, Stone Carrier, and Mother slept here. Stone Carrier's tools and the stone items he made took up the rest of the eight-by-ten-foot room. Shadow only slept in this room when Stone Carrier was away trading or gathering obsidian. Other times, she and Sun shared the small room directly above.

Shadow set her storage jug near the fire pit, debating about how much food she would take with her. Enough for two or three days, she decided. She would carry everything in Mother's large leather bag that she used for gathering plants.

Worry bit at Shadow as she studied Mother's medicine baskets, ceramic jars, and stone boxes. Her mother was depending on her to help with the birthing and had taught Shadow all the things to do when the time came. Mother was the only other person in the world besides Sun who loved and accepted her. With the baby due, this was not a good time to leave.

Shadow argued with herself. What she had felt all morning was not real. As Mother said, she just missed Sun. It was just her own fear and worry disguised as Sun's. Stone Carrier often said that her childish fears stole away her good sense. He was correct, of course, as he always was. Besides, Stone Carrier would never let anything happen to Sun. He and Sun were probably coming up the hill to the village at this very minute.

Sun's terror became Shadow's once more. She could not get her breath. Closing her eyes, Shadow felt Sun's lungs burn as he ran. Her legs felt his legs straining and his heart exploding.

The danger Sun faced was coming closer.

LITTLE SISTER." Mother touched Shadow's cheek. "What is it? You are as pale as a cloud."

Shadow struggled to catch her breath. Her tongue felt too thick to speak. She shook her head, and the room spun around her.

Mother felt Shadow's forehead. "Your skin is not warm or cold. Are you in pain?" She rolled out a yucca sleeping mat. "Lie down."

"I am sorry," Shadow mumbled, forcing her tongue to work. "I. . . ."

Mother pulled her down to the mat. "Rest. You are exhausted. You have done your work and Sun's since he left."

At the mention of Sun's name, Shadow's body shook. Mother knelt beside her, filling a ceramic mug with water from the large water jug. Sorting through her medicine basket, she pulled out a small leather pouch. Opening it, Mother poured bits of crushed plant into the mug and swirled it. She studied Shadow. "Drink this."

"I am not sick," Shadow tried to explain.

Mother nodded. "This will calm you." She pressed the cup into Shadow's hand. "Drink this. Close your eyes until I get back from taking Twisted Hair some pain medicine. Then we will discuss what is troubling you."

"Do you think the baby will come very soon?" Shadow reached up and touched her mother's bulging stomach. A gentle nudge from within greeted her hand.

Mother covered Shadow's hand with her own. "No, not today, tomorrow, or even the next four days. There is no need to worry. Old Child Bringer knows we may need her help." She squeezed Shadow's hand. "Child Bringer brought you and Sun into the world while in her old age. She will do the same for your sister, if needed. Now rest. I will take the medicine to Twisted Hair before the entire village suffers from her headache." With effort, Mother rose, carrying a pouch tied at the top. "I will hurry as fast as anyone can with Twisted Hair." She waddled to the door and out.

Shadow waited ten heartbeats and rolled off the mat. She snatched Mother's carrying bag from where it hung on a peg near the plants hung to dry. The deep bag was fashioned from heavy buckskin. A long flap covered the opening to keep water and dirt out. A thick shoulder strap made it easy to carry.

She studied Mother's collection of medicines, pain cures, stomach and bowel remedies, salve for cuts, tea to slow bleeding, and other remedies for countless ailments. For three summers Shadow had helped Mother gather plants, leaves, and grasses. Mother taught her to prepare and store them in various pouches, ceramic jars, and stone boxes while explaining their uses. If only Shadow knew what kind of trouble Sun faced, she would have better idea of which medicines to take.

Shadow selected a leather pouch containing herbs to slow bleeding. She debated on how to take the thick salve for open wounds. Mother always kept a large jar of it mixed and ready. The ceramic jar and lid were too large and heavy to haul. She needed something smaller, like a pouch. No, the skin would soak up the salve.

Her eyes rested on Mother's stone box as she contemplated. She fingered the delicate spiderweb-like design etched into its four sides. Such boxes, hewed from stone, were made by the desert people many days' travel to the south. The box's sides matched the length of her middle finger. The box's depth was a bit longer. The stone box was a gift from Stone Carrier, who bartered many spear points and stone tools in exchange for the box.

As she picked up the box, something rattled inside. Shadow slid the lid off and discovered Mother's shell bracelet, another gift traded for with the desert people. The white shell was acid-etched with delicate lines swirling into a geometric design. The graceful pattern suited Fair

Dawn perfectly. The expert workmanship made the bracelet beautiful and valuable. Mother only wore it on special occasions.

Shadow hesitated using the box, but decided that the salve was as valuable as the box. She nested the bracelet in a safe place within Mother's medicine basket. Using her fingers, she scooped the needed salve into the stone box. Shadow used a length of yucca cord to bind the lid tight to the box and slipped it into the gathering bag.

Moving to the cooking area, Shadow filled a dried gourd canteen with water from the water jar. Shadow grabbed a few strips of dried venison from a basket. With some cornmeal, she could make cakes and stew.

No. She would have to take a heavy ceramic cooking pot to heat it in.

Shadow took another handful of jerky and scooped some piñon nuts out of a yucca basket. She hated the thought of just dumping them into the gathering bag.

She spotted a round, white basket, another gift from Stone Carrier. It was the size of three fists with a lid that fit tight and a round knob on the lid that made it easy to open. Its small size and flat bottom were perfect for the gathering bag. Short strips of jerky and piñon nuts soon filled the basket, which rode neatly atop the stone box.

"Food and water," thought Shadow, slipping the gourd into the bag. She knew that she was forgetting something else—*Protection.*

Shadow crept to Stone Carrier's belongings. Her heart raced and her palms sweat. She was barred from this part of the room. Shadow lifted the lid of a ceramic storage container. Stone Carrier's "vision knife" rested inside. Shadow had only seen the long, strange-looking knife once before. When Sun had shown it to her, Stone Carrier had been away. They were six winters old then. This was before Stone Carrier took Sun to gather obsidian or on the many trips to other villages to trade.

"No one in the world has a knife like this one," Sun had confided. His dark eyes had shone beneath his straight bangs. He had Father's strong, square-shaped face and broad forehead. "Father saw this knife in a dream. Your fingers wrap around the long handle here."

"It looks funny."

Sun glared at her. "That is because you have never seen a weapon like this before. No one has. Other knives are shaped like a half-moon or a leaf that just rests in your palm."

"I know." It irritated her when Sun treated her like a baby.

"Father dreamt about this knife four times, four sacred times. On the fourth time, he knew the gods wanted him to make this knife!" Sun's face grew serious. "But they did not want it flaked from just ordinary obsidian. It had to be made from the most powerful stone in the world."

"How do you know?" Shadow demanded.

"Father told me. He has not told anyone else but me."

Shadow cocked an eye at Sun.

"And Mother, of course. Father found the stone on a mountain that only he has the courage to climb. Others are afraid to go there because a demon owns the mountain. Father is not afraid," Sun bragged, as he picked up the knife. It was twice as big as his hand. "Father prayed and fasted for days before he knapped the stone. With each chip, he prayed for guidance." Sun's voice dropped to a whisper. He clutched the knife. "It has special powers. I can feel them."

Shadow reached out to touch the vision knife.

Sun's free hand shot out, blocking hers. He swung the knife behind his back. "No. You know the law. No woman can touch a weapon." His eyes opened wider. "Lightening will shoot down out of the sky and burn you up, if you even breathe on this knife."

"I am not a woman," Shadow stated.

Sun set the forbidden weapon back into its container. "The law means girls, too."

"Mother does not die every time she cuts meat with her knife," Shadow persisted.

Sun closed the lid with a grating sound. "Mother's knife is not a weapon. It was not made to kill but to hack off meat after it has been killed."

"I see the no difference."

Sun his head. "That is because you are a girl."

Now, looking at the expertly formed knife, Shadow hoped Sun had been teasing. Her hands shook as she reached toward the vision knife.

Anyway, lightning could not shoot through the thick rock walls.

Her fingers touched the knife.

Nothing.

Shadow lifted the knife. The stone felt cold, hard—dead against her hand. Other than the way it sat in her hand and its weight, it did not feel any different than Mother's knife. The stone felt the same as her own stone scraper that she used to shuck off kernels of corn.

"It is just the same." Shadow placed the strange-looking knife in the bag. "Stone is stone."

She searched the room for anything else she might need. *Warmth.* Though the days were hot, nights brought numbing cold. Shadow grabbed a rabbit-skin blanket wrapped in a tight roll. It filled the last space in the bag. Perhaps she needed two. No, Stone Carrier and Sun carried their own in their journey supplies.

Shadow needed to let Mother know where she had gone, not to worry, and not to come after her.

Shadow thought for a minute, and images pecked into stone burst into her mind. Sun had taken her to see the "talking rocks" on Mother Mountain, west of the village. Pictures of birds, antelope, and snakes danced across one boulder. Drawn on other boulders were men hunting deer and dancing in straight lines. Only men chipped the images into the talking stones, but Sun and she had made pictures in the dirt many times. Shadow's figures looked more lifelike than Sun's. She enjoyed creating stories in the dirt. Sun could always decipher her pictures.

Shadow's eyes searched the room. Some of Stone Carrier's knapping tools, well-used pieces of antlers and horns, were wrapped in heavy pieces of leather. With care, Shadow undid a bundle and took the tools out. She carried the piece **15** of leather to the fire pit and squatted. She poked through the cold burnt logs till she found a charred stick that fit into her hand. Shadow spread the leather flat on the ground.

Time was running out. Mother would stop her if she came back.

Shadow pressed the charcoal stick against the leather and drew a circle with a dot in the center. Above the circle, she added a half circle for a brow. It looked enough like an eye for Mother to understand, Shadow thought. She sketched another bigger circle, this time with lines radiating from it. *Sun.*

The man bent under a bundle on his back was harder. Somehow it did look like Stone Carrier hauling his obsidian. Below these, Shadow drew a half-moon shape lying on its back. She added two dots for eyes, and a smile materialized. Shadow left the leather on the sleeping mat for Mother.

The sunlight made her squint after the dimness of the house. Shadow slung the gathering bag over her shoulder and scanned the plaza. Mother was not in sight. "Twisted Hair has trapped her with her endless complaints," Shadow thought. She darted into the passage leading out of the inner village. Anyone seeing her would think she was on a gathering errand for Mother.

No one spoke to Shadow. For the first time, she was glad that others usually looked through her or beyond her, as if she did not exist. She hurried through the outer rows of houses that dotted the hill. These stone houses had been built after those that formed the plaza, but even they were older than Mother's grandmother. Passing the last house, her stomach lurched.

"I have always wanted to travel far away from here, see new sights, have some excitement and adventure," Shadowed whispered to herself, trying to bolster her waning courage. "Now—now I am finally going to get my wish."

Shadow took a deep breath and scurried into the forest at the foot of Mother Mountain. Long, dark shadows swallowed her.

4

KEEPING TO THE FOOT of Mother Mountain, Shadow traveled north. The trees grew taller and thicker the farther away from the village she ventured. The sun stood directly overhead now, casting no shadows. Yet her twin brother's feelings clouded Shadow. Whatever danger Sun faced, it was drawing nearer to him. If only she could find Sun and help him. Shadow hurried along faster.

She reached into her waist pouch tied to her belt. The soft leather soothed Shadow's nerves. Mother had made the pouch, saying, "Take this to gather your yucca cords, pebbles, feathers, and other treasures in." She never scolded or scoffed at the boyish things Shadow chose to collect and cherish.

But then, Mother did not know about her kicking ball, a ball intended for male use only. Or did she? Shadow wondered, pulling the fist-sized ball out of her waist pouch. If Mother knew about the leather-covered kicking ball, she had never mentioned it. Shadow dropped it to the ground. It bounced. She cornered it between her sandaled feet and with a strong swipe kicked it ahead. Catching up to the ball, she whacked it again. It led the way through the forest.

"Many of the desert villages have great, open ball courts where men and boys compete with kicking balls. Women only watch the games," Sun had reported after a trading journey with Stone Carrier two summers ago. "The entire village goes to watch the games. I went, too. One group of men tried to boot the ball past the other group. It was exciting." His voice became serious. "It takes great skill to win."

"Some of the kicking balls are stone or wood," Sun had said. He held up a round shape covered in leather. "Others, like this one, are made of a hard, bouncy substance. I saw boys running and kicking them along the deep water canals that feed their corn and beans. One boy fell in and sank like a boulder."

Sun tossed the kicking ball up in the air and caught it as it came down. "I practiced kicking it all the way from the desert. Father says I am a strong kicker and an excellent runner. I am going to play in the boys' games next time we go."

With a crooked smile, he tossed the kicking ball to Shadow. "I will get another one for me." Soon, Shadow could run and kick as fast as Sun.

Now, Shadow booted the ball as hard as she could. With bouncing rolls, it challenged her to go onward, into the unknown world. "Please, guide me in the right direction," Shadow prayed.

Shadow visualized the images that Sun had drawn in the dirt one day last spring to show her where he and their father went to gather obsidian. First he drew Mother Mountain, near their village. Next, Sun sketched a larger mountain, the sacred Father Mountain. He scratched a line between the two landmarks and explained that they hiked through the middle of a wide valley between the two mountains. Then they traveled toward the sun's resting place until the valley ended. Some distance from the end of the valley, Sun drew a smaller mound.

He circled this brother-sized mountain. "We gather here mostly. The black stone found here is of good quality, and we know many good places." He lowered his voice. "This is not where Father harvests the best stone, the stone that has made him a respected man. No one knows where that is, except me." Sun's thin chest puffed out. "Someday, I will go with Father up Demon's Mountain and be honored, too."

After much pleading and swearing to secrecy, Shadow had learned the way to Demon's Mountain. "Once you leave the shadow of the Father Mountain, a lightning path leads the way," Sun whispered. Seeing Stone Carrier crossing the plaza toward them, Sun had erased his dirt diagram with a flash of his hand.

Lightning path. She had never heard of such a thing. Shadow booted the kicking ball, her frustration brewing.

She had been a fool not to have asked Sun what a lightning path was. She kicked the ball even harder. It hit something in the deep grass and sailed back at her.

She bent to snatch up the ball. The sound of movement nearby thrust her upright. Shadow peered around at the trees and rocks. The sound came again, in a hopping rhythm.

Shadow tried to scream, but only managed a squeak. She scrambled up a boulder. The rough rock broke her fingernails and peeled her bare knees. Her heart pounded, and her breath caught in her throat. She lay flat against the boulder's rounded top with her eyes pinched shut.

A harsh, rasping cry screeched through the air. Shadow stiffened against the boulder, but pried one eye open. With a whoosh of flapping wings, a black raven sailed into the air. The huge bird soared overhead. Cawing, it lost itself in the wind.

Tears of humiliation burned Shadow's eyes. A silly, old bird had sent her into a panic. If Sun had seen it, he would have laughed until he cried. And *she* was on her way to save *him* from some great danger. Shadow could almost hear her brother howling in delight.

She bit her bottom lip and shimmied down the boulder. Her knees felt weak, but she forced them to work.

Shadow seized her kicking ball, still lying in the dirt, and tucked it into her pouch. Somewhere, Sun faced unknown danger. For some reason, only she could help him. Shadow took one step, and then another. Nothing, especially her own silly fears, was going to stop her from helping her brother.

Father Mountain stared down at her. Shadow had lost track of time since her encounter with the raven. Now, a wide valley stood between her and Father Mountain. Shadow had never seen Father Mountain before but recognized it from the legendary, three jagged peaks forming a bowl of sorts at the top. She knew that the gods of her people slept in the hollow bowl of the mountain's top. Sun had said it was the tallest mountain in world.

Shadow jerked to a stop. Her throat ached with dryness.

She lifted the gourd canteen to her lips. The warm water twisted her stomach in hunger. Digging into her gathering bag for jerky, Shadow regarded the sky. The sun still had some way to go before it slept, yet the trees cast long shadows.

"I could stay here for the night." Shadow deliberated, chewing the dried meat. It tasted of smoke and salt. She concentrated on Sun's feelings, still threading through her. Shadow sprinted into the grassy valley. There was no time to waste.

The long grass bending over the rocky floor of the valley made running difficult. Sharp lava stones poked through the woven soles of her yucca sandals. Shadow slowed her pace. Watching for a safe place to spend the night, she wished that the sun would not sleep.

Shadow pushed on as far as the light permitted but did not make her way out of the long valley. A stand of tall trees with leaves quivering in a noisy dance beckoned to her in the last, graying moments of the day. The long grass beneath the singing trees would make a soft bed, Shadow decided. She wandered into the thick grove. The trees' white bark seemed to glow in the dying light. As she moved, Shadow gathered branches and twigs. A spark of excitement flared within her. It was time to test her fire making skill.

"Making fire is harder than just stirring hot coals in a house and more important," Sun had informed her many seasons ago. They had been hidden deep in the forest at the foot of their mountain. It was another one of the men's skills that Sun had taught her. "You must be able to make fire in a split second. Fire is the difference between life and death many times."

As always, Sun had been a patient teacher. Shadow found that he was correct: making fire *was* more difficult than just stoking the hot coals in a fire pit, as she had done so many times. It took many tries, twisting the fire stick in its notched-wood holder, to catch a flicker of fire on a bed of dry grass. Sun showed her how to breathe on the tiny, red spark, then to feed the spark so that it grew and became hungry for twigs, branches, and then logs. When

Shadow had finally succeeded in making fire, Sun forced her to repeat the feat twice, three times, and then four.

"I can do it," Shadow had stated, standing up with her hands on her narrow hips. "I am going to hunt piñon nuts. I am hungry."

Still squatting, Sun retorted, "You are always hungry—hungry to learn men's skills." He pulled his full lips together tight, and he looked like Stone Carrier.

"But I can make fire as well as any man now. It is easy."

Sun challenged. "Then make it faster than me."

After three contests and three losses, Shadow had continued to try to make fire. At last she could make it as fast as Sun. "Hide these in your waist pouch," Sun instructed, rewarding her with the fire stick and its holder.

Now, the memory of that day burned bright in Shadow's mind as she knelt to test her skills. Her hands trembled. The air suddenly seemed frigid as darkness swallowed the grove of trees. A red spark flew from Shadow's fire stick. It landed in the pile of dried grass below the stick's holder. With soft, sure breaths, Shadow began her fire.

"Thank you," she said, knowing the fire was her only shield against the black night. "Sun, thank you for teaching me."

A thick canopy of tree branches and leaves overhead masked the stars from Shadow. She curled down further under the rabbit-skin blanket, feeling safe beside her fire. Being alone in the darkness was not as bad as she had imagined. Why, it was sort of fun. If only Sun were here to share her fire.

Shadow closed her eyes, picturing Sun sitting next to Father safe beside a fire. But Sun's feelings of terror pushed the happy image aside and filled Shadow. Sun's heart raced so hard it hurt. An unearthly wail filled Sun's ears, stinging Shadow's ears at the same instant. White heat burned her lungs as Sun ran—ran from the wailing, snarling demon.

Now the unseen demon was right behind Sun. Shadow heard its heart thundering. She smelled its foul breath and felt its terrifying presence behind her brother.

"No!" Shadow leaped from her grassy nest.

She felt the demon sprinting inches from Sun.

"Sun, run! Do not try to fight it." Shadow's cries filled the aspen grove. The small fire licked the darkness, but did nothing to frighten off Sun's all-consuming terror. Shadow's body shook as she hugged herself. She tried to reach through the darkness and across the miles to her brother.

A searing pain slashed down the inside of her leg where it joined her body. Clutching her leg, she crumbled to the ground. Sun's physical pain surged through her. Her head spun in fuzziness. Sickness doubled-up her stomach.

"No," she mumbled as darkness cloaked her eyes, then her mind.

In a strange gray mist, Shadow floated miles above the Mother Earth. Emptiness bore into Shadow's body. The stillness of silence beat against her ears. Her heart ceased beating. No blood warmed her arms and legs. The air in her lungs staled.

Gazing at the earth's surface below her, Shadow knew that this was too real to be a mere dream. It was nothing like anything she had ever experienced before in the physical world that she lived in.

A vision. The realization burst into her mind. This was a vision, a personal message of some sort from the spirits, good or bad. Men told of such personal enlightenment sent to help guide and mold their lives or even warn of danger.

But only men had the privilege of visions, yet—

As Shadow's hollow shell drifted in the gray nothingness, lightning suddenly blazed around her. The lightning was not white or illuminating but a long, black snake's tongue that transmitted darkness and fear. A high-pitched wail rode on the lightning's drawn-out tail.

In another burst of black lightning, a form appeared. Its small, dark outline pulsated in and out. Lightning streaked around the form, spewing out darkness. The ghostly form became larger and larger as it consumed the lightning's dark power. Its howling vibrated within Shadow's heart. Somehow, Shadow knew that this growing, all-consuming form was the Spirit of Fear. *Fear,* an entity that took on endless shapes, forms, and guises, tried to steal life's breath from all it pursued. It was this Spirit of Fear, with its hideous cry, that stalked Sun.

The Spirit of Fear took the shape of a shadowy human figure in a long, dark robe of sorts. Its ghostly hands reached toward Shadow with long, skeleton fingers. A scream choked Shadow's throat. Her hollow shell could not move. The Spirit of Fear moved toward where she hung suspended in air, its wail turning to laughter.

With a clap of thunder, a brilliant red light filled the space between the Spirit of Fear and Shadow. Instantly, a woman's figure appeared. A flowing, red garment draped her strong body. Waist-long, dark hair swirled around her beautiful heart-shaped face. Her large eyes glowed with determination, and her finely formed chin angled upward in confidence.

The Spirit of Courage. Shadow recognized the woman in red and realized that Courage was the Spirit of Fear's greatest enemy.

The feminine Spirit of Courage faced the Spirit of Fear with open defiance, ready to battle. Shadow watched, her heart now beating in her throat.

A hate-filled roar rattled the air. The Spirit of Fear's human form whirled around and around, melting into a swirling dust devil. Now in the form of a huge cat, the Spirit of Fear pounced out of the funnel cloud toward the Spirit of Courage.

Seeing the black cat hurling toward her, the Spirit of Courage vanished.

Instantly, in midair, the Spirit of Fear's cat-form was jerked backward, controlled by some invisible force. The Spirit of Courage materialized, clutching the Spirit of Fear by its long cat's tail. With a graceful movement she twirled, swinging the Spirit of Fear by the tail in a wide circle. Her long dress floated around her like sunset-colored clouds.

Lightning flashed as the Spirit of Fear's cat shape vaporized with a deafening hiss.

A black lightning bolt soared toward the Spirit of

Courage and struck. The lightning burst into a black, glassy, tear-shaped bubble that encased the Spirit of Courage. In the center of the misty bubble, the Spirit of Courage pounded and lashed against the glassy force that held her prisoner.

The Spirit of Fear again transformed into a robed man-form. He seized the black bubble, which hardened into a stone with the Spirit of Courage trapped inside. Laughing, the Spirit of Fear hurled the tear-shaped stone downward.

The stone plunged to the ground. With a rumble, the earth shifted as the stone hit. The Spirit of Fear pointed to the spot. Black lightning shot from his finger, and a large rock formation, shaped like a crouching, guarding lizard, sprouted out of the ground. It entombed the stone, imprisoning the Spirit of Courage beneath it.

The Spirit of Fear whirled around, its skull-like face glaring at Shadow. Its skinless mouth grinned, and a long skeleton finger pointed at her.

WHEN DAYLIGHT BROKE, Shadow seized her gathering bag, scrambled out of her sleeping place, and bolted into the valley between the mountains. Her stomach twisted with anxiety and hunger. Her head ached from lack of restful sleep after experiencing her vision.

Cold bumps exploded up her spine and down her arms. Only men had visions, or at least only men reported having them. Perhaps she had just been asleep and the fierce battle between the spirits of fear and courage was just a dream.

Somehow it felt safer to think of the strange apparition as a nightmare instead of a message from the spirits. Visions were to be pondered, studied, and interpreted, but dreams were just cobwebs of the mind to be swept away.

Shadow focused her eyes on the grass before her to avoid looking at the sacred mountain, at her side. Custom ruled that women were not allowed on Father Mountain. Maybe sleeping so close to the holy mountain made her see— dream—such strange things. She pushed faster. Yes, that was the answer to her strange occurrence.

The valley emptied into a thick forest. Shadow scooted under the heavy ceiling of branches and out of sight of Father Mountain. Leaning against a huge pine tree, Shadow stopped to capture her breath.

As her heart and breath returned to normal rates, Shadow closed her eyes. She concentrated on the feelings filling her. Her knees buckled.

Her worries, anxieties, and fears were all hers. She felt nothing of Sun.

Shadow concentrated, trying harder to sense Sun's feelings at this instant, but still felt Sun's existence eclipsed from her; she no longer felt his presence within her own. She was cut off from him—severed in half. For the first time in her life she felt totally alone in the world. Tears stung her eyes and burned her cheeks.

"Sun, where are you? I need to feel you." Her cry echoed through the trees and lashed back into her face.

"Lightning path. I must find the lightning path. I am coming, Sun!" Shadow wiped her tears away and bolted between the trees.

Dry pine needles smothered the uneven ground. Chunks of rocks jutted through the needles. Fledgling pine trees and scraggly brush beaded the area. Nothing resembled a trail.

"Lightning path—lightning," Shadow mumbled, scurrying about. She wrenched her head upward. "Lightning comes from the sky."

The pine trees' tops nodded in the wind. Their branches waved down at her. A black scar singed into a tree caught Shadow's attention. She dashed forward, scanning other trees. The second burn mark, caused by a lightning strike, led her westward. It took longer to spot the third lightning-marked tree.

She vaulted over a rock in her way. "I found it, Sun. I am coming."

It took too many anxious minutes to detect the fourth scarred tree. The distance between lightning strikes stretched farther apart and became more difficult to ferret out.

"Please, please help me," Shadow prayed until she located the next mark.

The sun stood overhead when Shadow discovered the tall pine tree slashed from top to bottom by lightning. One half of the tree struggled to stand against the gentle breeze. The other half sprawled on the ground with its shattered branches rotting.

Shadow ran her fingers along the bare, splintered wood of the still-standing half. She stared down at the fallen portion, now in the shadow of its living part. Anger and sorrow clashed against each other for the same spot in her heart. The tree could not live very long without its fallen half.

Through the haze of her emotions, Shadow recognized the rock formation before her. Shaped like a giant lizard crouched on the ground, the rock guarded the end of the lightning path.

"The rock in my dream—vision," Shadow whispered to the torn tree.

A wailing shriek vibrated the air. Shadow grabbed the tree. The tree seemed to shudder. A second yowl thundered through the forest and rocks. The third screech sounded nearer.

Shadow spotted a dark opening in the ground situated just behind one of the lizard rock's front legs. She ripped her arms loose from the tree and forced her shaking legs toward the rock.

The unseen foe bellowed in anger.

She wormed her way into the narrow, dark opening. Cool, close air filled Shadow's nose and seeped into her lungs. The crevice broadened out a few inches from the opening. Shadow scooted on her belly, using her arms to pull herself into a small, dark chamber under the center of the rock. The rock rubbed the top of Shadow's head when she sat up, but she had plenty of room for her legs and arms when she lay down. She curled into a ball against the dirt and listened.

The animalistic cries and snarls circled the rock. Dark images stalked Shadow's mind with each outburst. This must be the demon that owned the mountain. Sun had never said exactly what kind of demon it was. It sounded monstrous, too huge to slither through the chamber's small opening. Still—

Shadow fumbled in the carrying bag, groping for Stone Carrier's vision knife. Clutching the hard, stone knife, Shadow shifted around on her stomach to face the opening.

"Please protect me," she prayed. Her hand sweated against the cold, stone knife.

Something on the ground beneath her gouged up at Shadow's chest. She rolled to her side and fingered the packed dirt, then felt a hard object half buried in the ground. Shadow dug around it and tugged it free. About the size of her hand, the object felt smooth yet strong.

Shadow held it up to the light seeping in from the small entrance. It was a tear-shaped obsidian stone.

The demon's angry scream pierced Shadow's body. She clutched the stone to her chest. Warmth and power radiated from the stone. Shadow's heart quickened.

Silence shrouded the dark chamber. Shadow strained to hear the wind dancing in the trees, the birds singing praises to Mother Earth, or the flying insects whispering secrets to one another.

She heard nothing.

Shadow waited, the knife in one hand, the other hand pressing the tear-shaped stone to her chest. The sensation of strength flowed from the stone into Shadow, nibbling away at her fear.

Time dragged by in silence.

The demon was waiting to spring at her when she wiggled out of her hiding place, Shadow decided. With each heartbeat, her eyes felt heavier. Her bones ached for sleep but her mind battled to stay alert. She rolled the tear-shaped stone over in her hand.

"I cannot stand it any longer." It seemed like days since the last cry. She needed fresh air and sunlight.

Squinting against the blazing light, Shadow slid out of her burrow. A bird's song welcomed her. A fly buzzed past her nose. The demon was gone.

Shadow examined the tear-shaped rock. Its thinness was deceptive of its strength. The tip of it was almost sharp to the touch. Below the tip the stone widened and smoothed into a rounded end. The sun glinted off its black, glassy surface. Flecks of red streaked deep within the thin stone.

Shadow held the stone up to the sunlight.

Within the glassy rock the image of a woman in long red garment appeared.

6

SHADOW STUDIED the red, female form imprisoned within the rock. The images of the night before streaked across her memory. A snake of coldness slithered up her back. Yet, the stone felt warm and strong and gave her courage.

Shadow's thoughts swarmed like bees around a hive. The notion that the strangely shaped piece of obsidian was the Stone of Courage buzzed loudest. She shook her head, trying to clear it. There was no time to think things through.

Slipping the stone inside her gathering bag, Shadow considered the mountain rising to the east. "Demon's Mountain." Her whisper startled her, and her heart skipped a beat. Here was the mountain only Stone Carrier dared to climb.

Somehow, Shadow knew Sun's courage had taken him up Demon's Mountain. Now, she too must trespass on it.

The first steps seemed impossible. The lava rocks under her sandals rolled and twisted. Perhaps the demon controlled every rock, tree, and bush comprising the small mountain.

Shadow's anger flared. Her imagination was taking over her good sense. Nothing had that kind of power.

Pine trees and brush grew thick at the base of the mountain. They thinned halfway up, where rocky ledges sprouted and climbed to the mountain's summit. Life struggled to grow out of the rocks. Sharp stones tore at Shadow's sandals and brush lashed her bare legs as she worked her way up the mountain's steep side.

Sun had said that Stone Carrier's secret quarry was near the top, on the setting-sun side. Shadow took the most direct course, the one she figured Sun would take. She searched for signs of Sun while struggling to keep her footing, but saw none.

She hunted in vain for some kind of path or animal trail. It was hopeless. No one could find anyone or anything in such a hostile and rugged place that the animals and birds avoided.

A steep ledge halted Shadow's steps. Her parched mouth shriveled tighter as she regarded the rocky barrier stretching in all directions before her. Shadow sipped from her canteen. She swirled the water around in her mouth and deliberated. Her legs ached, her heart pounded, and her anger broke.

"There is no time to go back." The sun told of midday. The possibility of being trapped on the mountain in the dark gnawed at her mind. This was no place to be in the dark.

Finding cracks and crevices in the rocks, Shadow inched upward. A cool breeze soothed her face. Sweat covered her hands, making it hard to get a firm grip. She felt sure that Sun had climbed here recently. Memories of him shimmying up the tall cliffs on Mother Mountain swarmed through Shadow's mind.

"It is easy, Shadow. One hand and then one foot," Sun had yelled down at her. They had been seven summers old. Sun had bragged that he could climb one of the steep rock walls near their village. Shadow watched him ascend like a skinny, brown spider. It looked so easy. Of course, she had gone up, too.

It had not been easy after all. Shadow found herself pressed tight against the rough rocks, her eyes locked on the ground below her. Terror raged within her like a wildfire.

Sun coaxed from above. "Look up at me, not at the ground."

"I cannot—I will fall." Below, the ground twisted and turned. Shadow's eyes blurred with tears.

"Yes, you can. You are being a girl-baby."

That was all Shadow needed to hear. Anger, drenched in determination, forced her up the incline. "Do not ever call me a girl-baby," Shadow growled, heaving herself up and over the wall. "I can do anything you can do, but better."

Sun had grinned. "I know."

"One foot then, one hand at a time," Shadow now repeated the advice spoken long ago. This ledge was easy compared to many of the cliffs Sun and she had egged each other up.

"Bet I climbed this faster than Sun." Shadow gloated, dusting off her hands. "Maybe we will just have to have a race, my brother."

Hollowness bore through her. She could not feel Sun's presence.

She worked her way around and up the mountain without a sign of Sun or Stone Carrier. Doubt wormed into her mind. "Maybe they did not come here," Shadow thought, nearing the top of the mountain. The lack of tracks or other signs supported her speculation. "Of course, that is why I cannot feel Sun. He is not here."

Hope surged against her worry. "Sun and Stone Carrier are probably at the village this minute. I cannot feel Sun's fear because he is safe with—"

The mountain shook with the demon's threatening wail.

The wail died, but its echo seemed to live forever. Shadow hurried to put distance between her and the cry.

Going down was more difficult than climbing up. Terror spurred her on and took over her reason. "Sun is not here," she cried. "Get off the mountain—get away from it!"

The demon's next angry squall caught her halfway down the mountain. It vibrated in every direction. Shadow ran faster, slipping and sliding. Even before the cry vanished, a second shriek pierced the air, followed by a third and fourth. The sounds came from all directions, only an eye blink apart. The demon was everywhere at once, but she could not see it anywhere.

The demon sounded like an animal. "A very angry animal," she decided, "or very hungry."

Yet, the screams, cries, and wails resonated with human meanings. If only she could see the thing.

Shadow jolted. A massive rock slide of boulders, rocks, brush, and small trees blanketed the mountainside. It appeared that some unseen power had shaken the mountainside like a feather.

Jerking around, Shadow realized that the only way down was to backtrack or go down through the unstable rubble. The demon's snarls thrust Shadow downward. Pebbles shifted and rolled under her weight. Rocks smashed against her ankles and feet. She hunched back and tried to slide with the rocks but fell flat on her behind.

The demon howled with delight.

Leaping up, Shadow toppled face forward. The avalanche of rocks and pain tumbled her downward. She struggled to push herself up and ride the wave of debris. Panic numbed the pain of smashing fingers, toes, legs, and arms.

Through tears, Shadow glimpsed a single pine tree bending under the weight of the landslide. Reaching out, Shadow wrapped herself around it.

The tree creaked and shuddered.

Shadow held tighter. She buried her face in the rough bark, praying for help.

The cracking and grinding of earth and rocks died. Shadow opened her eyes. The dust settled, leaving the air clear and quiet. Everything was rearranged. Now, the tree stood at the top of the slide area instead of in the middle.

Shadow gently pulled one leg free and then the other. Pain flamed in her body with each movement. Blood made her arms and legs a sticky mess. Grit coated her mouth and tongue.

Something caught her eye. Where the edge of the rock slide was originally, something that had been trapped under the slide moved.

The demon!

The brownish form moaned. The familiar-sounding groan stopped Shadow's flight. She peeked over her shoulder and reared around. Stumbling on shaking legs, Shadow made her way toward the dirty mass.

"Stone Carrier." Shadow knelt and gently turned her father over. Dirt encrusted his torn body. Dried blood glued his eyes shut. His right arm sprawled and twisted. Crashing, rolling rocks had mangled the fingers on his left hand, leaving a bloody clump. Shadow gulped down the queasiness rising in her throat. The cuts and bruises covering the rest of his body told of his burial under the landslide, and she wondered how he had survived.

"I am here." Shadow's tears washed his face. "Stone Carrier, I am here."

The man's head rolled. He struggled to open his blood-crusted eyes. "Sun—the demon. Run."

The demon's angry snarl rang between them.

$\mathcal{S}$un," Stone Carrier ordered, his voice laced in pain. "Go. Run."

"It is me, Shadow." She urged him to a sitting position.

Stone Carrier resisted, wrenching away. "Sun, leave me. Get away from the demon."

Shadow bit her lip. The familiar torment of not being seen, heard, or acknowledged by her father stung her heart like the open cuts on her arms and legs. "I will not leave you." She tugged harder. "But you have to help."

"No, my son. The demon has tasted your blood." Stone Carrier pushed Shadow's hands away. "It will not be satisfied until it has stolen your spirit."

A victory-like wail mocked Shadow's efforts. It sent her to her feet, ready to escape—escape the demon and her father's rejection. Stone Carrier was blind to her. She saw no reason to risk her life for *him*.

"Go, my only child. Go!" Stone Carrier cried.

Stone Carrier's words struck like lightning, igniting determined anger. Through gritted teeth, Shadow said, "I will not leave you." She pulled on him with all her strength. "I will not leave you until you see me. Hear me. And—"

The words "accept me" caught in her throat.

At the sound of her voice, Stone Carrier squinted up. "Sun?"

"Yes," Shadow strained harder. Let him think what he wanted. Obviously, he had made Sun leave him. But he could not force her to abandon him. She would stay beside him until . . .

The demon's taunting scream overshadowed her anger. Her body quivered like leaves in the wind. "Father, help me. I cannot face the demon alone." She heaved against his dead weight.

Stone Carrier groaned, pulling himself up. Shadow slipped her shoulder under his right arm. His left ankle dragged against the ground, unable to support his body.

"This way." Shadow battled to keep balanced on the sharp incline. Her anger somehow made her stronger.

The demon wailed in rage.

"If only I could see what I was facing," Shadow thought.

Within twenty steps, she sighted a hollow gouged out of stone at the foot of a rocky ledge. The opening appeared large enough for Stone Carrier yet small enough to barricade in some way. The scooped-out cavity itself was deep enough for them both to lie or sit and still have room for a small fire.

Fire. All animals feared fire. A fire would keep the demon at bay.

Stone Carrier moaned. Sweat scoured his pale, clammy skin.

"Just a few more steps. The gods provided a shelter," Shadow said, trying to keep upright.

"Nowhere is safe from the demon," Stone Carrier muttered. "It owns this mountain."

Shadow guided Stone Carrier into the hollow's small opening. "Duck your head." She helped him to a sitting position in the rocky cavity.

"Sun, leave me." Stone Carrier's voice faded. He slumped forward. His eyes closed.

Shadow put her fingers under his nose. Feeling breath, she maneuvered him to a lying position. She dug into her carrying bag for the gourd canteen. Somehow, the Stone of Courage tumbled out.

As if in response to the black stone, the demon bawled with anger.

Cold terror shook Shadow's body. As she held the black stone, unknown courage wrestled her fear, giving her strength.

The demon's shriek echoed off the rocks forming the hollow and died.

Shadow stared at the stone. The red streaks captured in its glassy shape appeared brighter, more distinctive. The woman's long, red dress seemed to sway. The notion that somehow the stone had frightened the demon nudged into Shadow's mind.

Stone Carrier moaned and shifted.

She slipped the Stone of Courage into her waist pouch. "As long as I have the stone, I will be safe."

Shadow marveled at Stone Carrier's survival as she examined his injuries from being buried under the rock slide. The crushing rocks left their marks on almost every inch of his body. His left ankle did not feel broken, but the way he dragged it convinced her that it was too twisted or torn for him to climb off the mountain soon. Three of his ribs felt misplaced or broken. With the slightest movement, bone scraped on bone in his lower right arm. This was Stone Carrier's chosen arm—the arm with which he carried the many bags of obsidian and threw his spear.

Shadow gently inspected the bloody fingers on his left hand. Grief pressed down on her. Without the mobility and strength in all of his fingers to hold his knapping stone, Stone Carrier's life as an expert stone knapper would end.

The many cuts and bruises covering Stone Carrier's body were not so serious, Shadow determined. The salve in the stone box would fight off the angry red flames and white ooze that foretold death.

Stone Carrier's ribs would be very sore and make movement painful. They would heal in their own way and time.

Shadow considered what to do about Stone Carrier's arm and fingers while she cleaned his other cuts with the water from her canteen. Broken and crushed bones were beyond her simple skills. At this minute she could not remember Mother ever teaching her about such injuries. Her thoughts began tumbling together in a wave of confusion and worry.

She took a deep breath to clear her thoughts and calm her jangled feelings.

Unnatural silence rang in her ears. The hair on her neck prickled. A deep feeling warned her that the demon was close, watching her every movement. If only Sun was here. He would know what to—

"Sun."

Doubt exploded in her mind. Sun would never desert Stone Carrier—never. Sun was as loyal to their father as he was to her.

Sun never disobeyed Stone Carrier, either. Stone Carrier's word meant law, and Sun avoided his father's anger as he would a rattlesnake. If Stone Carrier had ordered Sun to leave, then—

Apprehension swept Shadow's small frame. Where was her brother?

She concentrated on feeling Sun's presence—his being.

Shadow felt nothing but her own heart beating with worry.

Stone Carrier's words thrust into her memory. "Sun—the demon has tasted your blood."

8

STONE CARRIER moaned and thrashed. Shadow cupped his head to keep it from banging the stone wall. She whispered into his ear, "You must lie still so I can help you." His thrashing stopped.

Hunting through the gathering bag for medicine, Shadow's thoughts swam in turmoil. "I cannot think about Sun." A wave of nausea twisted her stomach. "I will not think about him now. One thing at a time," she told herself.

Shadow untied the cord around the stone box, removed the lid, and rubbed the thick salve into Stone Carrier's many cuts. With eyes closed, he responded to her hands with muffled groans.

Pressing her canteen to his swollen lips, she urged him to drink. He managed a few drops before slipping back into his world of pain.

Sitting back on her heels, Shadow sipped water. She added finding more water to her list of things to do. Caring for Stone Carrier's more serious injuries was the next thing on the list.

"No," Shadow stated, realizing how low the sun sat in the sky. "Keeping the demon out is first." She considered the opening to their cave-like hollow. Beyond, broken trees, brush, rocks, and boulders strewed the slide area.

After making a small fire near her father, Shadow covered him with her rabbit-skin blanket and crawled out of the crevice. The cool air shot a shiver up her spine. She hurried toward the rubble of the slide. Pieces of long, thin tree trunks, long limbs, and smaller branches angled up through the lake of rocks.

"I can stretch limbs and branches crisscross against the entrance," she decided. Shadow searched over her shoulder for the demon. "Then I will stack rocks in front of that to keep the demon out."

Her plan appeared easy. Carefully, she waded though the debris to reach a long pine limb. Pulling on it, the unsteady blanket of pebbles and rocks shifted under her. Cascades of small rocks tumbled downward. Shadow eased her way back to firm ground.

She decided to retrieve the long limbs captured in the edges of the slide. This forced her to scramble below the hollow and drag the heavy timber up the steep hillside.

Daylight faded too fast.

Shadow's legs and back screamed in pain. She wedged the last forked-limb into the tight web of branches and heavy boughs woven across the hollow's entrance.

Smoke from the fire near Stone Carrier seeped through the cracks in the barrier. The dancing fire provided just enough light for Shadow to see Stone Carrier's pale face. Beads of sweat glistened on his forehead and chest. His breath was slow and shallow.

"I am back," Shadow whispered. Her knees buckled, and she collapsed beside Stone Carrier. Clasped in her hand, the Stone of Courage radiated a feeling of security. "The demon cannot get us now." Her speech slurred. Fatigue numbed her body and crushed her eyelids. Her last thoughts were of Sun.

Twinkling stars searched for their brother the moon, sleeping behind the farthest mountain. The fire slowly died, and the demon roared in frustration.

A shaft of bright sunlight shot through the pine boughs, battering her closed eyes. Shadow turned her head from the light. Her head struck something hard. She sprang up and smacked the top of her head against the hollow's overhang.

Shadow went limp. Every inch of her body throbbed in stiff pain. As her mind tried to focus, the cuts and bruises covering her arms and legs stung in unison. Her mouth and throat felt dryer than sand.

"At least I know I am alive," Shadow mused, squeezing the Stone of Courage in her hand.

Alive—alive—alive. The words ricocheted around Shadow's mind as worry pumped through her body.

She rolled over and studied Stone Carrier. His chest moved slowly up and down. Shadow swallowed in relief.

Worry pressed down on her like the rock slide as she pulled herself up. Stone Carrier's head felt warm, but not hot. He did not respond to her touch. His mind hid itself from pain behind closed eyelids. Shadow checked the many cuts covered in ointment. They appeared well enough, but she would watch them closely.

Feeling Stone Carrier's swollen ankle, Shadow knew that it was just twisted bad enough to keep Stone Carrier off his feet for a few days. She hoped warm stones packed around the ankle would help ease the pain.

Shadow forced herself to gently inspect Stone Carrier's arm. She fought down the queasiness swirling in her empty stomach. The arm and the opposite hand swelled tight against the discolored skin.

Sifting through her memories, she tried to recall what mother had taught her about such injuries. No one in their village had broken a bone, she thought. But then a vague remembrance surfaced: Mother talking to someone. Child Bringer's face appeared in Shadow's mind. It was wise old Child Bringer that had taught Mother the healing skills.

"It was the only thing I could think of doing," her mother's words replayed in Shadow's mind. Fair Dawn was telling Child Bringer about a man from another village whom she had treated. "The arm was broken and bent. Left that way, he would never be able to use the arm again. I straightened the arm. The brave man cried out as I pushed the bone into place."

Mother paused. Grief reflected through her kind eyes. "His pain was my own. I bound the arm to a piece of flat wood like lacing a baby into a cradle board."

Child Bringer smiled, showing dark spaces instead of front teeth. "You did well, little sister. The wood will hold the bone in place while it mends itself. The strapping holding the arm must be adjusted each day."

The memory carried a wave of homesickness with it. Shadow wrapped her arms around herself. Tears stung her eyes. She wanted to be with Mother at home right now.

"Please let Sun be safe—safe at home," Shadow begged the gods.

As if Stone Carrier had felt her plea, he shifted. Shadow touched his cheek. He did not respond. The habitual hurt of not being acknowledged bore into Shadow like a hot arrow.

Later, Shadow was grateful that Stone Carrier lay with breath but not life.

"I will start with the broken fingers," Shadow thought, gathering her courage. She had scraped clean three stout twigs, a little larger than Stone Carrier's fingers. Lifting Stone Carrier's hand, Shadow checked his face.

No reaction.

Gently, Shadow tried to maneuver Stone Carrier's longest finger back into alignment. "Do not be stubborn," she said, applying force. Shadow laced the finger to its splint, with a strand of yucca cord from her waist pouch.

The finger next to his thumb gave Shadow more problems, refusing to take its original position. After many tries, Shadow bound it to the wood, knowing that it would never be quite right again. Stone Carrier's little finger slipped back into position with ease. It looked almost normal strapped to the splint.

"This is the best I can do," she told her unconscious father.

Doubt and worry curled like a snake inside her. "But it is not enough," she whispered. Nothing she ever did was good enough for Stone Carrier. He sought perfection in everything.

Shadow sighed and began manipulating Stone Carrier's arm. The bone's grinding brought bile to her throat. "I cannot do this," she cried, laying the arm down.

Her tears streamed down her face and over her lips. She licked them off. The salt singed her dry tongue. "Mother or old Child Bringer could not even fix his arm," Shadow thought. Best to just leave it.

Staring at the once strong arm, Shadow wiped her tears. If Stone Carrier could not use his arm, he could not quarry stone or shape it into knives, spearpoints, or tools. He would not be able to grow his corn or hunt. His pride would never allow him to ask for help or depend on others for food. Their family would starve.

Gritting her teeth, Shadow maneuvered the arm. "Please," she pleaded. "Guide the bone back to where it belongs." The bone slipped into place.

She used the last bit of her precious cordage to lash Stone Carrier's arm to a wide, smoothed branch.

"One more thing I need to do—make more cord," Shadow said out loud. Stone Carrier could not or *would not* hear her, but she needed to hear the sound of a voice, even if it was her own.

"I will check the lashings again in a while." Her stomach growled. Eating a strip of jerky, she studied her work. Stone Carrier's arm and fingers looked odd fastened to the bits of wood. Stone Carrier would be furious when he woke up and saw what she had done. He might even guess that she used *his* vision knife to cut and smooth the splints.

Two days ago, Shadow would have cowered at the thought of Stone Carrier's displeasure or anger. Now, she had more important things to worry about.

Staying alive was the most important.

9

GATHERING and then stacking large rocks against the wood barricade had taken Shadow longer than she planned. Now, the sun sat midway in the sky. Stepping back, she surveyed her completed work.

The hollow's entrance stood fortified and camouflaged. The web of limbs and branches crisscrossing the entrance supported the rock wall. Shadow left a small opening, just big enough to squeeze through. A pile of rocks waited inside to complete the blockade at night or in an emergency.

Her pride swelled, dimming the long hours of hard labor. The demon, whatever it was, could not possibly get through the rock and wood defense. She savored the taste of accomplishment. Even Stone Carrier could not find fault with her work.

Many times during the day, Shadow checked on him. Stone Carrier still breathed but had no wakening life. She packed warm stones around his ankle to help reduce the pain. Inspecting the lashings on his arm and fingers, Shadow saw that the swelling did not worsen. None of his cuts or scrapes appeared inflamed. Once, she coaxed water between his still lips, but the precious water dribbled out.

Shadow's own mouth turned to sand as she toiled. She tried not to think about the water in the canteen and had only taken one small sip. Her thirst surged and became unbearable.

She wiggled through the small opening into the shelter. Little showers of light trickled in between the cracks of the stones, branches, and pine boughs. Stone Carrier lay in the same, unchanged position. Shadow examined his injuries and detected no change.

Her eyes fell on the canteen siting next to him. She picked the canteen up and shook it.

"Just a few drops more." Shadow whispered. "I need to find more." Uneasiness writhed within her. To find more water required leaving Stone Carrier and the shelter's protection. But Stone Carrier needed water. His wounds needed cleaning again, as did hers.

Her overwhelming thirst confirmed that she had no choice but to go.

Shadow tucked the canteen into her gathering bag, wishing she had more than one vessel to hold water. The thought of the huge ceramic jars at home made her regret that she did not know the craft of pottery making. She shrugged. "Even if I was a master potter, there may not be enough water close by to fill even the canteen."

She knelt close to her father's ear. "I am going for water. You will be safe here. I will block up the opening from the outside." Shadow touched his cheek. He looked peaceful. A tenderness never felt before stole into Shadow's heart.

As Shadow hurried from the security of the shelter, she clutched Stone Carrier's vision knife in one hand and the Stone of Courage in the other. The stone fortified her more than the strange-looking, hard-to-hold knife. The air echoed deadly silence. She realized that she had not heard the demon since last night.

Perhaps it had left.

The hair on her scalp tightened. No, this was the demon's home. It would not abandon it. Shadow scanned the mountainside and saw nothing, but she knew the demon was watching.

Shadow wondered where the demon's territory and hunting grounds began and ended. She prayed that would it leave her alone once she got off its mountain.

She scurried into the deep forest at the mountain's base and strained to hear, to see, to smell, to feel her foe. Nothing seemed to exist in the world except her. Shadow sprinted on.

She concentrated on where to find water nearby. "If the demon drinks water, not just blood, there must be some water close." A shiver rattled her body at the notion of drinking the *demon's water*.

The lizard-shaped rock where she found the Stone of Courage suddenly stood before her. Shadow did not remember the rock being so close to the foot of the mountain. She leaned against the part of the rock that looked like the head of the lizard, and the memory of the night in the aspen grove flashed through her mind. Her vision replayed itself in vivid detail. Shadow felt sure that this was the rock in her vision. She stared at the glassy piece of obsidian in her hand. The Spirit of Courage had been imprisoned within just such a tear-shaped stone.

Shadow caught her breath, reliving the screams and wails of the Spirit of Fear. Somehow they reminded her of the demon's cries and laughter.

"No," she said, shaking herself back to reality and backing away from the lizard rock. "It is all too impossible—too frightening to even think about. I have to find water. Yes, find water." Even the difficult task of locating water was easier to face than piecing together what she had seen, lived through, and was experiencing now.

She knew that there was no water the way she had come to the mountain. So Shadow walked westward, her knees weak and her mind clouded in confusion. After a short distance, she realized the danger of getting lost and bent a branch as Sun always did when they explored new territory.

A sturdy yucca plant caught her eye, and she offered a prayer of thanks. The good spirits were with her. This was not a prime area for the spiky plants to grow, yet here was one for her to use.

The fibers of the sharp-tipped, sturdy, blade-shaped yucca leaves had countless uses: cordage, sandals, baskets, mats, needles and thread—even hair soap was made from yucca roots. Shadow swept her tangled hair from her eyes. The snarls felt as big as tumbleweeds. If only there were enough water to wash it. She decided to bind a bundle of the stiff yucca fibers into a hairbrush, if there were enough left after making the needed cordage. At least then she could comb out the tangles.

Shadow managed to hack off the broadest blades with Stone Carrier's knife. The yucca blades went into the gathering bag. She shoved the knife in with them, thankful to have 45 it out of her hand. The long handle fought her fingers and chafed her palm. "It is more like a fright knife than a dream knife," she mumbled, dropping the bag's flap in place.

Piñon nuts, unclaimed by the squirrels, lay under a scraggly tree. Shadow cracked some of the fingernail-sized nuts with her teeth. They tasted delicious. Her hunger slackened, but her thirst doubled. She harvested the rest of the nuts.

Shadow marked her way as she moved along. Seeing a patch of leafy plants, she sharpened the end of a thick stick. Stone Carrier's knife battled her every move. Shadow wished she had a conventional knife, one that fit her hand. The firm ground around the plants resisted digging, but the five round bulbs reaped were worth the effort.

"If only it was earlier in the season," Shadow thought. "There would be plenty of nuts, roots, and plants to gather." Realizing her ingratitude, she quickly offered a thanksgiving prayer for the food she had gleaned.

Shadow was not sure how far had she traveled, but she did not want to leave Stone Carrier alone too long. She picked up her pace. Shadow noticed a few other edible plants but did not stop to gather them. What she sought now was water. Later, she would come back.

"It is no use." Shadow's parched voice sounded like a toad's. She sank under a tree. Her thirst tortured every inch of her mouth. She clamped her eyes shut and leaned against the tree. What a fool she had been to think that she could find water.

The hair on her neck prickled. Something was watching her.

Shadow's eyes popped open.

Something moved in the thick trees to her left. Shadow sprang up. At the same instant, a doe, followed by a yearling, leaped past her and darted off into the trees to the north.

She gasped for breath and saw the well-worn path between the vegetation. Shadow bent another branch and followed.

The narrow path wound down a ravine and then out again. It ended at the base of a pine-covered mountain larger than the demon's. Shadow smelled water. Her legs suddenly had a mind of their own, pumping toward the sweet, wet aroma.

Tall trees and grass encircled the spring that trickled out of a mound of rocks. A small drinking hole formed below. On her stomach, Shadow lapped the cool, sweet water till her stomach felt like bursting. She rolled over on her back. The trees shared their shade. The knee-high grass offered a soft bed.

"Thank you," she prayed.

Her eyes felt heavy. Somewhere a bird called out. A second bird answered and began a soothing melody. Shadow turned over and gulped more water. A sense of peace swelled her heart. It would be wonderful to spend the rest of the day lying here. If only Sun was here to share it with her.

At the thought, her peace shattered. She considered trying to feel Sun's emotions. The fear of feeling *nothing* stopped her.

"Sun is at home, safe with Mother," she tried to convince herself. Rolling over, she began filling the canteen. Doubt and worry nagged on, eating at her mind.

Shadow's legs began to shake as she started up Demon's Mountain. The demon's threatening wails warned her not to tread any farther. She gripped the Stone of Courage and continued climbing.

The unseen demon screamed in anger.

"I am back," Shadow whispered to Stone Carrier. He had not moved an inch.

The demon's shrill howling shook the walls of their shelter. Shadow tried to ignore the shrieking. "I found water." She kept talking even though Stone Carrier remained asleep. "I gathered food and yucca. I will make snares with the cordage I twist from the yucca. Roasted rabbit sounds delicious."

Shadow examined her father's arm and fingers. "I need to adjust the lashings on your arm. With the fresh water, I will clean your cuts again and put more medicine on   **47** them." Shadow worked gently, but quickly, hoping he would not wake until after she finished.

Shadow thought about what she would say when Stone Carrier did wake up.

She shrugged her shoulders. It did not matter what she said—Stone Carrier always refused to hear her.

Hurt and shame washed over Shadow.

10

THE DEMON TORMENTED Shadow with its howls the entire day as she worked, sitting just outside the barricade. She did not see the demon but felt its eyes watching her every move. There was no doubt in her mind that the demon was a tangible, living, breathing, thinking thing with uncanny powers. Somehow it seem to know what she was doing and thinking, even what she was planning. The demon did not show itself, but it expressed itself clearly.

Shadow discerned expressions, tones, and emotions in the demon's voice. It mocked her in laughter-like shrieks as she tended Stone Carrier's wound. "You fool. He is mine. I have tasted his blood," the demon seemed to declare.

All day Stone Carrier hibernated in lifeless sleep. Now and then, he called Sun's name. Shadow tried to wake him. Comfort him. Give him water. Nothing worked. He sank deeper into his unnatural sleep.

The demon's voice claimed, "Mine. He is mine—mine—mine!"

As Shadow chewed the last piece of her jerky, the demon basked in victory. "Hunger will twist your stomach now."

It became a game, a puzzle, Shadow interpreting the demon's language of wails, snarls, and cries. The burning need to understand the unseen foe flamed hot. The more she comprehended, the better she could fight it.

Dissecting the demon's language in her mind, Shadow pounded the yucca blades. Pent-up tension spewed out with each smack of her stone. The crushed blades lay with the strong fibers exposed.

Shadow separated the long, wet yucca fibers with her fingertips and gnawed along an edge of a cut blade. It flavored her tongue with a green freshness. She rolled two long bunches of fibers back and forth on her thigh. The left hand moved the fibers up, while the right hand glided them down. The opposing motions twisted and warped the fibers into a strong cord. As the cord grew in length, she added a few more fibers at a time.

The demon responded in contempt.

She wove and tied the long cords into a netlike snare, and the demon raged. When her knots broke, the demon jeered. "Silly girl. Silly girl. . . ."

The game stretched on after the stars lit the sky. Shadow spent most of the night, curled in a tight ball, listening to the demon's taunting calls.

When grays and pinks tinged the morning sky, Shadow left her shelter and closed its hole with rocks. The demon's threatening taunts followed her down the mountain, warning her not to return. At any second she expected the demon to lunge. Shadow clutched Stone Carrier's knife in her right hand. In her left, she embraced the Stone of Courage. The stone sustained Shadow's spirit, but her thin legs still could not carry her fast enough off the mountain.

Now, the empty canteen swung from its strap on her left shoulder. The gathering bag lopped from her right shoulder, stuffed with yucca blades, three handfuls of piñon nuts, and a huge clump of edible leafy greens. A sense of calm refreshed Shadow as the echoed memories of the demon's voice faded with each step.

Shadow hunted for a place to set her snares. An area covered with low brush and weeds caught her attention.

"There," she thought, moving to the area. "Rabbits travel this way to get water." Neat little piles of rabbit droppings confirmed her speculation.

Taking a yucca snare from her gathering bag, she tested each knot. Shadow remembered Sun doing this last spring. Her mind's eye brimmed with the memory.

Sun had squatted deep in grass, not far from the village. His long, black hair, bound at his neck, glistened in the sunlight. "You must hide the snare so the rabbits cannot see it."

Shadow had knelt beside him. She watched closely as Sun looped the ends of the snares into place. It looked easy enough. "Let me set the next one."

"You know the law," Sun said. "Women cannot hunt meat."

"But *I* gathered and pounded the yucca. *I* tied the snare." Shadow snapped.

Sun nodded. "And your snare is stronger than mine."

"Then let me set it."

"No," Sun's intelligent eyes looked as stern as Stone Carrier's. "Punishment will fall on both of us."

Shadow stamped her foot. "Punishment has never stopped you from teaching me things before."

"I know." His stony face mellowed for a breath, then he shook his head. "This is different somehow. I will show you how, but it must be *my* hands that set the snare."

Despite Shadow's pleading and loud threats, Sun had set the snare. Step by step, time after time, he displayed the skill. Bored, she had tromped off.

Now, Shadow wished that she had practiced what she had seen. There was so much to remember, and that day seemed a lifetime ago. She knelt in the heavy undergrowth and twisted the snare's net out on the ground. After three tries it finally looked correct. Shadow crimped the long anchor ends around stout brush stalks. She set her second snare close by.

Anxiety choked her as she filled the canteen at the spring. Shadow questioned the strength of her knots and if her snares were secured firmly. Visions of furry rabbits sitting on their fat haunches, laughing at her snares, flashed in her mind.

"Please let the snares work," she prayed. Her stomach added its own plea in a loud rumble.

A cloud of small birds darkened the sky. Shadow peered up at them as she wedged the wood stopper into the canteen's opening. Memories of Mother roasting such birds on a spit danced before her eyes. Remembered smells teased her nose. Her stomach snarled and grumbled. With cupped hands, Shadow gulped more water to quench her stomach's demands. She wondered what Sun and Mother were eating for breakfast.

Coldness, as frigid as the hardened water in the winter, stiffened Shadow's body.

Sun. . . .

She reassured herself that Sun was safe at the village with Mother.

Why, by now she could have a baby sister.

Doubt blurred her thoughts. Hunger twisted her stomach, and worry slashed her mind. Mother had counted on *her* to help deliver the baby. Sun would be useless in childbirth, and old Child Bringer's eyes could barely see.

Shadow's back went rigid. She was wasting precious time trying to help someone who did not love or even accept her. Mother needed her, wanted her. Stone Carrier did not.

"If I leave now and run all the way," Shadow calculated, "I can be home before the new day."

Deep in her mind, a small voice confided, "And you would not have to face the demon."

Thundering hooves crashed through the trees. Throaty growls and howls vibrated close behind. The smell of death burned Shadow's nose.

11

A HUGE BUCK EXPLODED out of the trees. Seeing Shadow, it lurched. A large rack of antlers weighed on its head. Its chest heaved in and out. White, foamy saliva dripped from its strong, sensitive mouth.

For an instant, the animal's soft, brown eyes met Shadow's eyes. They pleaded for help while warning her of danger.

Shadow's heart tightened.

The buck veered and leaped, kicking up pebbles and dust. Shadow dove behind a fat tree.

Snarling and growling, two, three, four gray, furry shapes sailed by the tree.

Shadow raced in the opposite direction. She dodged branches and swooped over brush. The baying of wolves as they surrounded and killed their prey came within twenty heartbeats. The hair on Shadow's neck stood on end. Her legs pumped harder.

The image of the buck glared in Shadow's mind. The look in its eyes reminded her of Stone Carrier's gaze when she had first found him. His words repeated themselves in a ghostly echo. "Leave me. Get away from the demon."

The buck had led the pack of wolves away from its off-spring. Shadow felt sure that the animal had sacrificed itself for the safety of the doe and fawn she saw yesterday.

Shadow's breath caught in her throat. This was part of being a male: facing uncertainty, fear, even death for your family. Nausea swept over her. Stone Carrier risked his safety every time he left the village to gather obsidian or to trade with other villages. He risked his life for not only Mother and Sun but for her as well.

As daylight began to fade, Shadow finished placing the last stone in the entrance. When she turned around, Stone Carrier's dark eyes stared at her.

"Stone Carrier," she said, crawling. Her relief surged. He was awake, and she was no longer alone.

His eyes gazed up and right through her.

Hurt seared Shadow. She wanted to turn away—run away.

Outside, the demon screamed in delight, as if to say, "He does not see you because he does not want you."

Hearing the demon's taunt, terror streaked across Stone Carrier's face. His body went rigid.

"We are safe," Shadow forced the words out. She touched his shoulder. He flinched from her touch.

"It cannot get to us. I made a wall of wood and stone." Shadow uncorked the canteen and slid her hand behind Stone Carrier's neck. Raising his head, she guided the gourd to his cracked lips. "You need water."

Stone Carrier tried to lift his right arm. He moaned and stared down at it.

"Your arm was broken—crooked." Her wariness of Stone Carrier snarled her tongue. "I—I—the wood will hold the bone in place while it heals."

Stone Carrier studied his wood-bound arm. His eyes widened when he caught sight of his left hand.

"I did the same thing with your fingers," Shadow explained, waiting for his anger.

The small fire popped.

Stone Carrier closed his eyes.

"No. Do not go back to sleep. Do not leave me again." If he went back to sleep now, he would never wake again. "You must drink." Shadow held the canteen to his mouth. Her fingers trembled. "I—I found a spring. It is a small one, but it is sweet."

After three deep swallows, Stone Carrier laid his head back. His eyes began to close.

"I found a few piñon nuts," Shadow offered, trying to

keep him awake.

The walls of the shelter quaked with the demon's thunderous wail.

A nervous laugh escaped Shadow. "The demon is mad because you are awake—because you are alive."

Stone Carrier stared at her for a heartbeat, then turned his eyes to his surroundings.

Shadow watched her father survey the barricade. Pine needles had begun to drop from the wood, but the limbs held firm. In the fire-lit darkness, their shelter was small, yet secure. Shadow realized that Stone Carrier was now staring at the dancing fire.

The hair on Shadow's neck prickled up. Of course, he would now realize that she knew how to make fire. Her eyes found the ground and waited for Stone Carrier's wrath.

With a loud crackle, the fire swayed.

Shadow felt Stone Carrier's eyes on her. Out of respect and intimidation she kept her eyes lowered.

Silence bore into Shadow's heart—silence and rejection. Tears stung her eyes. She fought them back. Stone Carrier hated weakness. Well, he would not see weakness in her, even if he did look at her. Anger shoved at Shadow's hurt.

Straightening her shoulders and tossing her head, Shadow glared at Stone Carrier. His eyes saw only the fire.

"The canteen is here if you want more water." She plunked it down beside him. He did not move. "If you need anything else . . ." Shadow's voice quivered, then broke.

She knew Stone Carrier's ears and eyes were closed to her.

12

SHADOW'S PLEASANT DREAM melted away like ice, too
rapidly for Shadow to catch and remember as she pried
open her eyes. She stretched her cramped legs. The chill of
the autumn morning chafed her bare shoulders and arms.
She wound into a tight ball for warmth.

Not even a single red ember flickered in the fire pit.
Shadow glared at the cold ashes. Closing her eyes, she
willed the fire to blaze, to give off life-sustaining heat.

"I wish I had brought two blankets," she thought behind
her closed eyelids. Her rabbit blanket wrapped Stone Carrier snugly. Wishes burst into her mind like the stars that
sailed through the night sky. A mug of hot mint tea teas-
ingly offered tasty warmth. Of course, one needed a pot to
cook the tea in and a mug to drink it from. Shadow wished
for not just one cooking pot, but two. She fancied a deep
bowl for stew—rabbit stew.

Next, Shadow wished for her long, leather leggings and
heavy shawl. A pair of warm moccasins that fit her feet like
her own skin became her next desire. The corners of her
lips tickled. "Finely crafted moccasins." Shadow pictured a
whisper-soft pair. Bright colored beads formed intricate
swirls and whirls on the white doeskin.

"I will dance in them, and the other girls will be jealous."

Homesickness welled up within and trickled over. A
salty tear slipped between Shadow's parted lips. She opened
her eyes to a teary blur.

"Wishes are like the stars; easy to see, impossible to
grasp," she whispered. The words were Stone Carrier's,
mandated to Sun many times. Stone Carrier believed only
in reality.

Swallowing her homesickness, Shadow scooted to the lifeless fire. She used her fire stick and dried pine needles from

the barricade to ignite a fire. Feeding the small, hungry flames, Shadow glanced over her shoulder. Stone Carrier's eyes stared at the fire, then darted to her face. For an instant, Shadow thought she saw recognition. Before she could speak or move, Stone Carrier gazed at the fire again. Hurt, edged in red anger, warmed Shadow's body, and she bit her tongue to keep the angry words in her mouth. She preferred Stone Carrier's wrath to his rejection.

Shadow hoisted the canteen to Stone Carrier's mouth. He took a few swallows without sound. His eyes avoided her.

"The swelling is less in your fingers," Shadow said, only in her mind. She gently inspected each finger and adjusted each lacing. Stone Carrier held his body rigid as she worked.

"Your arm is swollen tight. Does it hurt terribly?" Again, no words left Shadow's mouth, just echoed in her mind.

Stone Carrier's ankle appeared the same. "I will pack warm rocks around it again today." Her words tumbled about her mind in loud, clear tones, but the shelter remained as quiet as a tomb. "You must try to put weight on it. The sooner you can walk the sooner we can leave this place."

Stone Carrier stared into the fire as Shadow probed his ribs. As far as she could tell, they were mending. Scabs protected the cuts and scrapes.

Pride spilled into Shadow's heart. Mother would be proud. The image of her mother brought a new wave of homesickness and worry.

Shadow turned away before her tears tumbled down her checks. She wiggled out of the shelter. Cold air whipped her face. Shadow slumped against the barricade. Hot tears cascaded down her face.

"Why should I stay here with you?" she whispered between sobs. "Why?"

The demon's voice ruptured the nippy morning air. "Leave—leave him. He is mine," it seemed to say.

"No," Shadow screamed back. "I will not leave him to *you!*"

Stone Carrier sipped water, but his stomach refused the piñon nuts. His flesh hung on his body, and his cheeks hollowed from lack of food. Shadow knew that he could not survive on mere drops of water. Perhaps his stomach would accept tea. There were many plants she could use; bitterroot, mint, serviceberry, or even some—

Shadow scolded herself. Without a cooking container, there would be no tea.

She positioned the canteen at Stone Carrier's lips again. He drank without looking at her. His eyes closed. Shadow sat back on her heels and watched his chest moved in the rhythm of sleep.

"Perhaps his lack of emotion or speech is caused by his injuries," Shadow thought, positioning the fire-warmed stones about his ankle. Mother had spoken of people whose bodies existed here while their spirits dwelled in some unseen world.

"I wish I knew," Shadow said out loud. She remembered her morning wishes and laughed. Only the cooking vessels seemed important now.

Shadow's stomach growled at the thought of hot food. Somehow, she must devise something to cook in. This was one wish that she must make come true.

The first snare was as she had left it, except for fresh rabbit droppings nearby. Her frustration boiled. If only the rabbit had gotten just a bit closer.

She dashed to the next snare and found it torn into two pieces. Tangled in one half was brown rabbit fur. She scooped up the broken strands of yucca and studied it.

Sitting by the spring, Shadow tested each knot as she made a new snare. She chewed on a slice of root. It was stringy with age, but tasted passable.

"I have retied every knot and tested each three times," she said to hear the sound of a voice. "No rabbit will break this snare." The taste of roasted rabbit tormented her mouth. Rabbit broth would provide Stone Carrier strength.

"I will set this snare in a different spot, where it will surprise the rabbits. There might be a place beyond the spring." The lure of exploring new territory sparked her excitement. Not far from the spring, she discovered an excellent site. "Please," she prayed, leaving the snare, "guide brother rabbit here. Please let the trap work this time."

The afternoon sun shone warmly. White, billowing clouds speckled the sky. Birds and insects harmonized lazily.

"If only I did not have to go back." Shadow's feet slowed. "Back to the demon's taunts and Stone Carrier's cold silence."

Tears pricked Shadow's eyes. Weariness clawed at her body. The thought of the demon's unseen eyes observing her buckled her knees. She grasped a pine tree for support. Shadow doubted that the demon would let her come and go from its mountain much longer. When its deadly attack came, she would have no way to fight the unseen demon.

"I do not want to go back." Shadow clenched her fist. "I do not have to go—"

Her fingers stuck together. Standing free of the tree, Shadow glared at the gooey mess on her fingers and palm with anger and frustration.

"Pine pitch. I will never get it off; it will stick to everything I touch. I wish that—" She pinched her thumb and longest finger together, and her mind whirled. "My falling star—a wish come true." Shadow rummaged in her gathering bag. Using her clean hand, she selected two of the broadest yucca blades that she had gleaned earlier.

"All I have to do is scrape the pitch off the tree and onto the yucca blades." She hesitated at the thought of using Stone Carrier's vision knife for such a messy job.

"What will he say if he finds out?" Shadow whispered.

Defiance struck. "Nothing. Because he does not talk to me."

With the tip of the knife, she scraped a gob of pitch off the rough bark. Long, sticking tendrils clung to the tree as she transferred it to a yucca leaf. "This will not be easy," Shadow muttered.

She just hoped it would be worth it.

THE THICK HANDLE of Stone Carrier's vision knife stuck to Shadow's pine-pitch smeared hand. She carefully carried the pitch-covered yucca blades in her other gooey hand. The full gathering bag cuffed her right side. The replenished canteen bounced on her left side.

The demon's voice railed when Shadow entered its territory. "Why do you try my patience, silly child?" it seemed to say.

Fear flooded Shadow. This could not go on much longer, the demon letting her trespass just to taunt her. There had to be a reason why it had not killed her the instant she set foot on its mountain. It must want something, Shadow decided, but she had no idea what.

Shadow set the yucca blades, canteen, and gathering bag outside the barricade and hid the vision knife in the bottom of the bag. Uncovering her crawl-hole, she peered in. She felt Stone Carrier's eyes watching her from within the dim shelter.

"I am back," she called through the widening hole. Her sticky hands clung to each rock. Wiggling into the shelter, Shadow watched Stone Carrier's eyes turn to the smoldering fire.

Anger sprang up, and she bit her tongue. Shadow whipped her back to Stone Carrier and tugged the canteen into the shelter.

"It is easy for you to look away, but I will not make it so easy for you to shut out my voice," the words exploded in her head.

Shadow swung around. "I brought fresh water." Her voice sounded shallow.

Stone Carrier avoided Shadow's face as he sipped from the canteen she held.

"Your ankle looks better." Shadow's voice rang through the shelter.

She prattled on in a tight, too-loud voice. "The sky is collecting clouds. It will rain soon." Shadow adjusted the lacings on Stone Carrier's broken arm. "The harvest feast is today. Everyone will get drenched, including Spring Breeze, who thinks she will dance with Sun this day."

At Sun's name, Stone Carrier's body stiffened. He clamped his eyes shut. His pale face twisted in anguish as he turned it to face the wall.

A wave of alarm crashed around Shadow, silencing her.

Something was wrong, wrong with Sun.

She dumped the few remaining piñon nuts out of the yucca basket and hurried out of the shelter without looking at Stone Carrier.

Gulping in fresh air, Shadow battled her apprehension. "I am being foolish again. Sun is at the village, safe. Why, Spring Breeze is probably flapping her eyelashes at him this very minute."

The demon's hideous laughter sliced the humid air.

Shadow stood her ground. "Sun is safe," she cried. "You are just mad because he escaped you."

Wailing jeers resounded around the mountain.

"And we will, too!" Shadow shouted over the demon's shrieks. "We will escape." Confidence rang in her voice, but her knees fluttered like blowing grass. The round storage basket twitched in her hands. Only her sticky fingers kept it in her grip.

To show the demon and to still her quaking knees, Shadow plopped down. "I am not afraid of you." Her sticky hands dug into her waist-pouch and found the tear-shaped Stone of Courage. Its touch bolstered her determination. Pulling it out, Shadow held the stone to the sun. The red-streaked form seemed to sway with gentle elegance in its stone prison. Shadow watched in fascination.

A long, angry howl shook the mountain like thunder. It rolled off rocks and trembled trees. As suddenly as the blare began, it vanished. Deadly silence rang through the air.

Coldness crept up Shadow's back. She clutched the Stone of Courage. Warmth and strength swept the coldness away.

Shadow placed the stone in her lap and lifted the yucca **61** basket's tight lid off. She eyed its interior, the size of three fists. "Large enough for two mugs," Shadow chuckled. "No, three boxes of tea."

She wondered why she had not considered the basket before now. Ceramic pots were the first choice for cooking since they could be placed directly over the fire, which allowed food to be cooked fast and steaming-hot. Yet, baskets had served as cooking vessels long before ceramic ware did. Hunters and travelers carried lightweight, unbreakable baskets for cooking in. Hot stones plunked into the basket heated its contents.

Thinking of hot tea, Shadow's mouth watered. "Not just tea, anything I can find, I can cook." Her voice filled the quiet air, and her thoughts swirled.

The small, expertly woven basket had a graceful shape, never meant for cooking. "I need something to spread the pitch around the inside with to make it watertight."

The basket was five inches deep. Her fisted hand fit comfortably through the basket's four-inch round opening. Using Stone Carrier's large knife would be impossible.

"I need something that just fits in my fingers." Shadow felt the inside of the basket. "Something with a wide, strong edge to spread the pitch evenly. It must have a steep edge, like a hide scraper, so it will not cut the basket."

Shadow deliberated. "Maybe I can find a stone that will work."

Her search for a stone near the shelter proved worthless. Shadow widened her quest to the rock slide. "This is impossible. Every stone is too big, too wide, too thick, or too little. None of them have the right kind of edge." Shadow thrust her hands on her hips and glared at the rubble before her. Large, dirt-covered chunks of obsidian caught her eye.

"Of course." Shadow picked up an obsidian slab. "I can make a scraper. I have watched Stone Carrier chip tools all my life. Even Sun makes scrapers, so it can not be that hard. If Sun can do it, then I can, too." As she spoke, nervous anxiety snaked in and out of her mind.

Tradition proclaimed the privilege of flaking stone into

tools and weapons as men's right. Women only used the stone tools that men made. The idea of a woman flaking stone was unthinkable. When Sun began learning his father's trade, Shadow had not even thought to ask him to share this knowledge.

Here and now though, traditions seemed remote and distant. Apprehension tweaked at her mind.

Shadow hurried back to the shelter with a large core of obsidian and an oval hammer stone. Sitting down near the entrance, she took a deep breath and placed the core stone on her lap. It was the size of both her hands folded together.

Her stomach knotted up in a tight ball as she considered the rock. "If only I had Stone Carrier's flaking tools."

She picked up the smooth oval, granite rock. Her fingers did not quite wrap all the way around it as Stone Carrier's fingers did around his hammer stones. She hoped it did not matter. If there were rules or creeds governing every aspect of flaking stone, then she would most likely break everyone of them.

Shadow fingered the edges, ridges, and sides of the obsidian. She concentrated on the stone, pushing her fears and doubts aside. "I can do this. It is just a scraper, nothing more. I need to break off a flake that will fit into the basket's opening."

She turned the core stone over and over, debating on where to start.

"Here, where three sides join with a ridge running down the middle. But first, Stone Carrier always smoothes the corner down." She rubbed the hammer stone against the edge where the sides joined.

"Now I just need to hit it here." She aimed the hammer stone just behind the smoothed-off corner and came down with a hard whack. The ridge line of the stone fell off into her hand in a long piece.

"I did it. It was easy." She turned the thin flake over and disappointment bore into her. "It is too long. I know. I will break it down to the right size. If I hit it right here, it should—"

63

The thin flake broke into two, but not as Shadow envisioned.

Picking up the two small pieces, Shadow shook her head. "They are still too big, and if I break them down anymore the edges will be lost."

She bit her lip in frustration and picked up the core piece of obsidian again. "This time, I will strike farther from the corner."

It took two blows to chink out a wide flake. It was shorter and thicker than the first. Shadow tested it. The flake fit her fingers and went through the basket's opening with ease. Shadow touched the flake's fine edge.

"Ouch!" Shadow sucked her finger and tasted blood. The edge would slit the yucca basket as easily as her flesh. The flake needed the edge her hide-scraper had. The steep edge scraped the hair off, without cutting the hide itself.

"There must be a way I can make the right kind of edge." Shadow mulled over Stone Carrier's techniques. Hammer stones chinked off flakes, but pieces of deer antlers performed the precise job of making the different types of edges.

Tension stretched her mind as she pondered her options. "Perhaps I can just dull the edge with the hammer stone."

With careful motions, Shadow rasped the hammer stone along the flake's edge. It looked better, but was not exactly what she needed. She would just tap the hammer stone ever so gently along the edge to make it deeper.

The hammer stone chinked a gap in the edge.

"No." Shadow cried and hurled the useless obsidian. Tiny knife points pricked at her eyes. "I will do this."

She snatched up the core of obsidian. "I will do this if it takes an entire mountain of obsidian."

The darkening sky lit up with a web of lightning. Thunder crackled. Shadow held the stone scraper in her fingers. It felt comfortable. She tested how it fit inside the basket.

Twisting her fingers, the scraper's edge glided along the inside of the basket without nicking it.

"I did it. I made a scraper." Her failures, a mound of obsidian flakes, sat next to her. "And next time it will not take me all day."

A deafening clap of thunder shot Shadow to her feet. She collected everything into her gathering bag, except the pitch-covered yucca spears. The bag went through the crawl-hole first. She carefully dropped the yucca into the shelter next.

Lightning flashed, and Shadow squeezed through the opening of the shelter as huge drops of rain splattered.

Shadow fed the fire to a bright glow. Hunching near the light, Shadow drew pitch onto the edge of her scraper. Carefully, she worked the scraper through the basket's opening. She started with the basket's bottom first, smoothing a layer of pitch onto it. The pitch lumped into a glob. Shadow pried it off and started over. Again, the pitch clumped and rolled together.

Frustration consumed her. "There has to be an easier way—a trick to doing this," she thought.

The fire snapped.

"Maybe if I heat the pitch just a bit."

The sound of thunder agreed with her whispered words.

Taking a clump of pitch on the scraper, she held it as close to the fire as she could. "Just enough to soften the pitch."

Shadow smoothed the warmed pitch inside the basket. "Better, much better." She heated more pitch, this time a little longer, until the scraper felt warm.

She hummed as she worked on the sides of the basket. A flash of lightning glowed outside. Thunder rattled the shelter. Shadow continued humming but suddenly felt Stone Carrier's eyes stabbing her. Her heart skipped a beat. He must have heard her making the scraper. She paused, her hand hiding the tool inside the basket.

Thunder rolled into the shelter between the branches and rocks.

Shadow hummed and withdrew her hand from the

65

basket. From the corner of her eye, she saw Stone Carrier gape at the scraper. Fear clogged her throat. Maybe she should she beg for his forgiveness.

"It would do no good," she thought, heating more pitch. The hair on the back of her neck stood on end. Stone Carrier witnessed her every move but said nothing.

"There, that will do," Shadow thought with pride. She set the basket down. "The pitch should dry by morning. Maybe I should put two coats of pitch on it." She rubbed an itch on her chin.

Her eyes wandered to Stone Carrier. His face was toward the back wall.

Shadow sighed. "Even when I do wrong, he refuses to see me. There is no reason to even try. Why should I stay?"

She stared at Stone Carrier. A feeling somewhere between love and hate filled her heart.

"Because I am his daughter, and I am just as stubborn as he is."

14

LEAVE ME!"

The agony-laced shriek shattered Shadow's cozy dream of devouring steaming rabbit stew with Sun. Before she could open her heavy eyelids, Stone Carrier's anguish and fear screamed against the darkness.

"Run. Save yourself. Go."

The terror in Stone Carrier's voice spread fright-bumps over Shadow's body.

Lightning flashed outside. Thunder shook the shelter.

Stone Carrier sobbed, "My child."

Groping in the dark, Shadow stripped a handful of pine needles from the barrier. Bright flames sprang up where she pitched them into the hot coals. Stone Carrier thrashed on the ground. Shadow shoved a branch into the flames and scurried to him.

With eyes closed, grief gnarled his features into a horrifying mask. Tears surged down his sunken cheeks. He jabbed at an unseen fiend, wood-bound fingers bobbing. His splintered arm smashed against the ground. "Take me. Eat my flesh, but leave my child alone."

"Stop." Shadow clutched Stone Carrier's shoulders. "It is just a dream."

Lightning brightened the shelter. Stone Carrier's tormented eyes glared into Shadow's. He struggled up, thrusting her aside. "Go, leave me. Leave me before the demon kills you, too!"

Shadow sprung back and shook her father. "It was a dream, just a nightmare. Please, Father."

Stone Carrier's body slackened in her arms. Shadow's arm tightened around him, and she eased him back to the ground.

"Not a dream," Stone Carrier mumbled. He stared up at

Shadow. "I forbade Sun to climb the mountain. I ordered him to stay away no matter what he saw or heard."

Shadow's body numbed with disbelief. Stone Carrier's words melted into a swirling nightmare. Her heart rammed her ribs.

"Sun heard the demon's cry and came searching for me." Intensity carved Stone Carrier's voice. "Sun thought that the demon was attacking me. He came to save me." Stone Carrier clamped his eyes tight, sobs racking him.

Shadow needed to scream, "Stop! It is not true. I will not let this be true." But her tongue stuck to the top of her dry mouth. Her windpipe squeezed shut.

"The demon," Stone Carrier's eyes widened with the memory. "Blood spurted from Sun's thigh. I could not stop it. I tried everything I knew, but the blood kept flowing." The flickering fire reflected the pain in Stone Carrier's eyes that tears could never wash away. "I held my son, watched his life drain away, and could do nothing to save him."

Thunder roared.

Shadow became stone. Her mind and heart rejected what her ears heard. Her eyes refused tears. As long as she did not cry, it would not be true. As long as she did not cry, Sun would be alive.

The fire burned itself out.

Shadow coiled into a tight ball in the darkness. Squeezing her eyelids together, she dammed the threatening tears. "It is not true. It is not true," she whispered over and over.

Scalding tears beat against Shadow's closed lids. She fought them, somehow keeping Sun alive and well. Her eyes stung with a thousand bee stings. She battled them back. Shadow would not let Sun die with her silly tears.

"It is a dream—a nightmare. I will wake up and Sun— Sun will be—Oh, Sun."

Against her will, despair-filled tears cascaded down her face.

In the cold darkness of the night, Shadow cried. She cried for Sun, who would never again walk by her side. She wept for Mother, who would carry her sorrow in silence. She lamented for Stone Carrier, racked in remorse. She wailed for herself, left to face the world without her brother's companionship and love.

Shadow cried until there were no more tears left in the world.

The lightning-laced night skulked into a gray morning. Shadow, eyes swollen-dry, climbed out of the shelter without a glance at Stone Carrier.

Outside the cold, damp air pierced her bare legs and shoulders. The earth appeared as dead as the murky sky overhead. Light penetrated the thick clouds, but the sun hid its face.

Shadow's body felt hollow. She had to concentrate and struggle to accomplish the simplest movement. Each breath of air burned her lungs. Every thought was as slow as mud. Each step down the mountain became twenty.

Tear-like drops of water seeped from the tall pines as Shadow shuffled beneath them. The trees' tears splattered her head and dribbled down her shoulders. She did not notice. The wet grass drenched her sandals and chilled her feet. She did not care.

In a gray haze, Shadow wondered why she was going for water.

Because it was what she always did. There was strange comfort in routine. The realization punctuated the cold reality that she needed to be away from Stone Carrier. *He* was responsible for Sun's death. It was Stone Carrier who had insisted that Sun go with him to quarry obsidian. It was all *his* fault.

Anger could not permeate Shadow's empty body. Even if it was Stone Carrier's fault, it did not matter now.

"Sun is dead," Shadow whispered.

Her heart ripped in half.

In a louder voice, Shadow repeated the painful words. "Sun is dead."

"My brother is dead!" Shadow's scream echoed everywhere and nowhere. "Sun is dead and nothing can change that."

69

Her shrieks ricocheted back to her ears. Her heart heard the words and accepted them.

It was true.

It was true. Nothing could change what had happened.

Nothing would bring Sun back to her.

Nothing.

The spring overflowed its pool from the rain. Bubbles burped out of the canteen's submerged opening as water rushed in. Shadow watched the round air bubbles float to the surface, rupture, and vanish.

"This is what death is like." Shadow's perceptions were sharper now. "Your spirit bursts out of your body and just disappears."

Shadow's head became too heavy, and she drew her knees up, wrapped her arms around them, and cradled her chin on them. She contemplated the canteen filling itself on the pool's bottom. Another bubble surged to the surface. The bubble did not rupture but skimmed the spring's glassy surface in graceful delight. Its watery dome reflected the clearing sky.

Shadow squeezed her eyes shut, not wanting to see the bubble's death.

To her people, death was part of living; the final step in this world, the initial stride into the next. For the first time, Shadow questioned the teaching of the next-life, where spirits dwelled in the House of the Dead somewhere on Father Mountain.

What did spirits look like?

She could only picture Sun with his long, black hair flowing behind him as his strong legs ran. Straight teeth gleamed. Dark eyes sparkled as he smiled in her mind. His laughter rang in her ears.

She wondered if spirits felt pain or sorrow but hoped that there was only happiness and joy living on the sacred Father Mountain as a spirit. If only she knew what Sun was doing and thinking at this instant.

A moan ripped from Shadow's heart.

What if there was no House of the Dead—no spirit life?

Perhaps death was just empty, black nothingness. Weariness overpowered Shadow in a dark vapor. She did not have the energy or the will to ponder it all now.

Later, when she was home safe, she would seek the answers to her questions and worries.

Shadow felt the sun's rays warming her back. The warmth spread through her body. She lifted her head from her knees. The sun greeted her face with gentle heat.

"Please, just let me go home—home with my father," she prayed. "Let us find peace within our hearts and with each other."

Her legs felt so weak that she debated checking the new snare. The snare's distance stretched endless. Tomorrow she would check it.

Tomorrow—there might not be a tomorrow.

There would never be a tomorrow for Sun.

Today was the only day she could count on. She dragged herself up and lumbered in the direction of the new snare.

Shadow squinted. Her heart sped up. She rubbed her swollen-dry eyes and stared again at the snare. A mound of fur lay within the snare's tangled grip. Shadow moved closer. The rabbit was motionless. Claw marks dug deep into the earth represented the creature's battle against the yucca cords.

Shadow knelt next to the still animal. "Your heart must have burst under your struggle."

Sorrow ripped Shadow as she stroked the velvet fur. "I am sorry, brother rabbit." Warmth rose from the rabbit, as if its spirit lingered near. "You offer my father strength. Thank you. I will not forget."

Shadow sat beside the rock barrier in the warm sun. She grappled with Stone Carrier's vision knife trying to skin the rabbit's pelt from its body.

The strange knife fought her every move. It seemed to know that Shadow had no right to use it. Her fingers slipped. The knife jabbed deep into her left palm. Blood oozed.

"I need my own knife, a knife that fits my hand and obeys me." Shadow said. "If only I could—"

She whisked away the notion of making a knife. Making a stone scraper was one thing, but knapping a weapon was not an option—yet. Blisters, nicks, and cuts would be the price she paid for using the vision knife.

After what seemed like forever, the rabbit's pelt crumpled to the ground. Screwing the entire rabbit onto the cooking spit she had made presented its own challenge. Finally, Shadow used yucca cords to help bind the meat in place.

"These will hold long enough," Shadow stated. The sound of her own voice gave her comfort. "Just long enough to brown the meat. Then I will strip off the meat and cook it in a broth in the basket. I should have checked the basket before I left to see if it was dry or not."

Shame burned her checks. She had not bothered to check on Stone Carrier either.

The shelter was cold and damp. Stone Carrier faced the wall. Shadow's heart tightened. It had been wrong not to care for him before she left.

She touched his shoulder.

He stiffened.

"I brought fresh water."

Stone Carrier shifted his head.

"The rain added its freshness and strength to the water." Shadow pressed the canteen to his lips. "I should have lit the fire before I left. I am sorry. I will start one now."

Stone Carrier's good hand covered Shadow's hand. "I am sorry." His voice was as quiet as bat wings in the night. "I am sorry I did not keep your brother safe." His dark eyes glassed over with tears.

Shadow's chin quivered. Her throat tightened. She fought back the tears as she nodded.

Stone Carrier squeezed her hand with unknown gentleness.

15

THE FLAMES SPRANG UP around the drops of rabbit grease drizzling from the spit. Smoke, warmth, and the aroma of roasting rabbit swelled the shelter. Shadow's stomach roared, and her mouth drooled. She rotated the wood spit, held up between two forked stick-holders, over the small fire.

"Not long now," she said, glancing over her shoulder. Stone Carrier's sleeping face was free from pain. Shadow nudged close to tuck the blanket over his exposed shoulder. She touched his cheek ever so gently, remembering how his tears and hers had run together. Their hearts had beat in unison, grieving for Sun.

Scooting back to the fire, Shadow shifted the meat again. She inspected the stones heating at the edge of the fire. "I had best start warming the water so it will be hot when I add the bits of meat."

The water in the basket hissed as she carefully dropped in a hot stone. A cloud of steam drifted up from the basket. Half full of water, it accommodated only one heated stone. Shadow waited until the stone cooled. Using two sticks, she worked the stone out of the basket and plopped another hot stone in. The cool one went back into the fire to reheat.

Shadow dipped her fingertip into the heating water. "Just a few more stones and it will be hot enough for bits of meat." The process was tedious compared to cooking in a ceramic pot.

A flat stone became her cutting board. The sizzling meat burned Shadow's fingers as she sliced off a small piece. Again, Stone Carrier's vision knife refused to cooperate. It slipped and wiggled in her greasy fingers. Dropping bits of rabbit meat into the basket, Shadow licked her fingers. The smoky flavor of rabbit taunted her tongue.

Shadow was tempted to eat the next piece, but she dunked it into the basket. Her stomach rebutted with a loud growl. Shadow added more small bits of meat and plunked another hot rock into the basket. Pushing the lid in place, she put the basket aside to let the broth simmer.

She tussled with the knife to carve off the rest of the meat. "I will save it for the next batch of broth." Her stomach grumbled, begging for just a taste.

The knife rebelled as she slashed off the dark meat. With an incredible twisting spiral, Stone Carrier's vision knife dove into the middle of the hot flames with a dull thud.

Tiny red sparks spewed up. Orange flames pranced around the black knife. Shadow whipped around to see if Stone Carrier saw.

All Stone Carrier saw were his dreams. Shadow prayed they were pleasant ones, not like the one she was living at this minute.

Shadow selected the longest branch in the wood pile. After four attempts, she jostled the knife from the fire's grip. The fire scorched the hairs on her arms and charred her face. She glared at the knife. "You would burn me good if I picked you up now. You may be Stone Carrier's dream knife, but to me you are nothing but a nightmare."

She yanked up the remaining meat. "I will not give you the chance to hurt me again." Shadow bit a hunk of meat off and chewed. She took a second bite and a third, glaring at the knife with anger.

Only after devouring every scrap of meat off of the bones did Shadow's anger numb. She scowled at the pitifully small pile of stripped-clean bones, all that remained of the rabbit.

Shame engulfed her.

"Forgive me." She bowed her head. "Forgive me for being greedy—thoughtless of our future needs." One small basket of broth would not restore Stone Carrier's strength. She needed the good spirits to lead more rabbits to her snare.

Suddenly the demon's laughter rattled the shelter as if it had seen everything. "You greedy child, I have you now—

both of you."

Shadow dove for Stone Carrier's knife, snatching it up. Burning heat seared her fingers and palm. She flung the knife down. Its hot tip struck the flat cutting stone and ruptured.

The demon taunted in a shrill wail, "Soon you will be my meat."

"I will not!" Shadow screamed voicelessly and tugged the tear-shaped Stone of Courage from her waist pouch. Its warmth somehow soothed her blistered fingers. She held the stone up before her. In the fire's glow, the arms of the imprisoned woman reached out in comfort. Courage and strength flowed from her outstretched arms.

An unnatural hush penetrated the shelter as the demon's voice ceased.

The fire forgot to pop and hiss.

Studying the strange piece of obsidian, Shadow wondered at its strange power to silence the demon. Somehow the Stone of Courage was keeping them safe—for the time being, at least.

Shadow doused the broken knife with the last drops of water from her canteen. The tip of the knife was ruined beyond repair. Large nicks gouged the once sharp edge. She burned with dread and shame. "Even the stone cannot give me enough courage to tell Stone Carrier about this," Shadow admitted to herself.

She stashed the ruined knife in the bottom of the gathering bag. "I will bury it when I go for water."

"Shadow." Stone Carrier's drowsy voice startled her.

She slapped the bag's flap down. "Yes?"

Stone Carrier pressed upward. "The demon—did you hear the demon?"

"Yes, but we are safe here." She helped him to a sitting position.

"No," Stone Carrier stared into Shadow's eyes. "No one is safe from it. Leave me, go now."

Shadow glared back into her father's frightened eyes. "I will not."

"I order you to leave."

"When I leave, you will go with me."

Stone Carrier roared, "I cannot walk."

"Not until you try," Shadow said in just as loud a voice. "Are you refusing to try?"

Stone Carrier flinched. He forced his splinted-fingers up. "I cannot hold a spear or even a knife."

"Well, I can!" The words exploded from Shadow's mouth.

Shocked silence, both Stone Carrier's and Shadow's, bore deep into the shelter.

Shadow swallowed hard. Her mouth felt dry, gritty, her tongue thick. "I—I made broth. See if your stomach will hold it."

Stone Carrier's lips parted, then clamped shut. The muscles in his jaw strained. His eyes snapped closed for one heartbeat, then five. He jarred his head, almost a nod. His eyelids lifted.

In his eyes, Shadow saw a swirling pool of frustrated acceptance. Her heart quivered with sorrow and understanding. She bit her lip, lowered her eyes, and slid to the fire.

The basket felt warm to the touch. Shadow lifted the lid, and steam puffed out. She removed the cooking stone with the sticks, then cleared her throat and picked up the now empty, stone medicine box.

She maneuvered close to Stone Carrier, balancing the basket and box. She poured broth into the square stone box and set the basket aside. "This will be easier to drink from than the basket." Shadow held the box to her father's lips.

Stone Carrier drank. His dark eyes stared at her over the edge of the box. After three swallows, he paused, pushing the box away. He opened his mouth to speak.

Shadow's heart raced. Her eyes squeezed tight, waiting for the interrogation about who killed the rabbit. She shuddered in anticipation of his anger. Warm broth sloshed over her hands.

Somehow the box steadied. Opening her eyes, Shadow saw Stone Carrier's splinted-fingers supporting the trembling box. He steered the box to his lips and drank again.

Shadow felt a wave of pride. Stone Carrier was trying to

use his hurt fingers. They were mending. Her efforts were working.

For the second time in the day, Shadow went for fresh water. Her mind whirled with the events of the morning. First came accepting Sun's death, then finding the rabbit in her snare. She replayed the moments spent weeping with her father. Fear-bumps covered her neck as she thought about breaking Stone Carrier's knife. Confusion flooded her mind when she relived the confrontation with Stone Carrier and his silence over the rabbit meat.

The events swirled in her mind like a cloud of dust that the wind twists, turns, and skips along the ground. She strove to sort things out, put them in a meaningful order. It was useless. Her mind and heart refused to work together, each having their own ways and desires.

She tugged her feet to a stop. A rabbit lay dead in her first snare.

Her mind rejoiced. The good spirits had provided more food.

Her heart sank in sorrow. Another rabbit had died that they might live.

Her heart and mind battled each other.

Questions leaped into her mind. Both creatures had died in her snares, which was odd. Usually, rabbits were just trapped by snares, not killed. Yet she had not been called upon to actually *kill* the trapped creatures.

Shadow put the fat rabbit in the gathering bag. "Some good spirit is helping me." And she offered a prayer of thanks, hoping she was correct.

Filling the canteen at the spring, Shadow muddled over her obvious problem. The rabbit needed cleaning and skinning, soon. She had no knife to do it with. Without a knife, the meat was useless, a mockery to the animal's death. Without a knife, hunger stalked their every breath. Without a knife, death crept closer.

A chill writhed around and up Shadow's backbone.

She had no choice. Whether she wanted to or not, she needed a knife. There was only one way to get the needed tool and weapon: make it.

Shadow wonder if even the good spirits would permit such disregard and mockery of the age-old creed.

16

WITH SWEATY HANDS, Shadow reset her snare in a new location. The words of the age-old hunting song drummed in her head.

> We hunt and kill our animal brothers,
> That we might live another day.
> Their flesh becomes our flesh,
> Their strength becomes our strength.
> To waste their life-sustaining meat,
> Brings dishonor and hunger to all.

The rest of the song dwindled from her memory. Shadow thought of the slain rabbit in her gathering bag. She shut her eyes, asking which is the greater sin: wasting meat or making a knife?

No answer came, except hunger worming in her stomach.

Opening her eyes, she caught a glimpse of bones half hidden in the undergrowth under the trees.

Shadow studied the bones strewn in a wide arc not far from her snare's new location. "It is the buck that the wolves were hunting," Shadow realized.

The stripped-clean rib cage and backbone lay under the tree. Even the sturdy hide had been ingested. Now she understood why wolf and coyote scat often appeared furry.

The buck's front leg bones were yards apart. Shadow spied the top part of a hind leg under another tree. The lower part was missing. "A wolf carried it off to gnaw on elsewhere," she deduced. Whatever the wolves had not devoured, the coyotes, ravens, flies, and nature's other scavengers had.

Shadow's heart coiled with sorrow as she remembered the buck's dignity and beauty. Apprehension rimmed her sorrow when she recalled the stark fear burning in the buck's eyes.

So, this was death; fear and then scattered white bones.

The eyeless skull glared up at Shadow. A narrow ring of brown fur gripped one multi-pronged antler in place.

"An antler—flaking tools." Shadow's mind overpowered her grieving heart.

The antler was too long to stash in the gathering bag. She would hand-carry it. Shadow sorted out the bones. "I can grind down the pelvic bone for a platter."

Her thoughts jumbled with excitement as her hands harvested. "I can make awls for sewing, a scoop for serving, smaller scoops for eating, a hair comb—" The fuzz on her neck prickled like porcupine quills.

"But, first I must make a knife."

The cool grass beside the spring cradled the rabbit's stiffened body. Time pressed upon Shadow's shoulders. She could not put it off any longer. Shadow rubbed the dirt off the large chunk of obsidian. The stone's dull black skin hid its glassy-keen beauty. Her hand trembled. The spring rippled encouragement.

"Please forgive me. If my father and I are to live, we must eat. To eat, I must have a knife." She hoped the listening gods had hearts as understanding as the good spirits that had provided the flaking tool.

Still, with all her soul, Shadow wished she did not have to break the time-honored creed.

"*Life is too precious to cast off in the name of customs.*" Mother's words came to mind as plain as the bird's song overhead. A tight, aching lump clogged Shadow's throat. If only Mother were here to—

Shadow gritted her teeth and blinked away her sudden tears. "Life is too precious to cast off in the name of customs." She lifted up the obsidian core. In the other hand, she gripped her hammer stone.

Stone Carrier's instructions to Sun resounded in her memory. "*Your heart and eyes must guide your hands. The stone will comply when you see in your heart what your*
hands are to make."

Shadow pictured her knife. It did not have a strange handle like Stone Carrier's vision knife, now buried deep in the soft earth by the spring. Her knife was the typical leaf-shape. She visualized the rounded end fitting snugly in her palm. The keen edge and tapering end obeyed her fingers' every whim. Shadow rotated the knife in her mind to observe, and study each groove, strike mark, and gouge. Her eyes scrutinized the uncut stone in her hand and compared it to the knife in her mind's eye.

"Please guide my hands, my heart, that we may live." With the hammer stone, she struck the core behind a long ridge line. A neat chip flaked off in the shape Shadow had pictured. She held her breath and studied the flake.

It was perfect, for the first step.

Setting down the hammer stone, Shadow took up a spike-tip that was broken from the antler. She must now create the keen edge used for skinning and cutting the rabbit's meat. Shadow positioned the antler.

The image of her knife burned in her mind as a prayer sang in her heart.

Stone Carrier leaned against the back wall as Shadow wiggled into the shelter. The shelter was dim and cold. Worry trenched deep valleys in his face and vibrated his voice. "I was afraid that you . . ."

"I am sorry it took so long." Shadow plopped her gathering bag down and stoked the fire to life. She slid close to him with the canteen.

He held up his crippled left hand as Shadow lifted the canteen. With clumsy effort, he hoisted his splinted broken arm up also. His unharmed fingers wrapped around the canteen. His splintered fingers added support and led the canteen to his lips. After a deep swallow, Stone Carrier managed to lower the canteen to his lap. "You look like your mother when you smile like that."

"You held the canteen, alone." Shadow took Stone Carrier's mangled hand. "The swelling in your fingers is gone. Do they hurt much?"

Stone Carrier shrugged. "Only when I move them."

"The sticks must stay on. The bones have not healed completely, but they are mending straight. You will be able to use them again." Shadow checked his broken arm and adjusted the yucca lashings. "It may take longer for your arm to mend, but it will not be misshapen either. How do your ribs feel?"

"Painful, especially when you poke them like that."

Shadow caught her breath. "I am—I was just—"

"I know." Stone Carrier's voice softened like the autumn's sun. "I am sorry, too. It is not your fault that . . . "

Shadow saw tears cloud Stone Carrier's eyes. "It is not yours, either," she said.

Stone Carrier turned his eyes to the fire.

The popping of the fire echoed about the shelter. The cold air began to warm around Stone Carrier and Shadow.

"I will find you a walking stick tomorrow," Shadow said, after a long while.

Stone Carrier nodded. Tears glistened on his checks.

Shadow busied herself at the fire with the rabbit. She had cleaned and skinned it at the stream with her new knife. The rabbit pelt stretched over a rock outside, along with the other skin. This rabbit was fatter than the first, yet it went on the spit easier.

"I am learning," Shadow thought, resting the spit on the forked sticks at either side of the fire. "I am learning so much."

Her knife lay beside the Stone of Courage and the ball in her waist pouch. It turned out shorter than she had pictured, but it fit her hand with comfort. The tip and edge lacked the honed sharpness of Stone Carrier's knives, yet it cut well enough to skin and clean the rabbit.

It was far from a weapon to fear. This fact made Shadow feel less guilty, but still unprotected. Somehow she must make a weapon to protect them. But right now, her knife would help provide food for their stomachs.

Stone Carrier retreated deep into his thoughts as the rabbit cooked. Shadow turned her back so he could not see her

sneak the knife out of the waist pouch. It felt good in her

hand. Its edge peeled the meat from the bone while nestling in her palm. She cut the rabbit legs off and what meat she could, then slipped the knife into her waist pouch.

"I added piñon nuts and some herbs to the broth." Shadow held the stone box to Stone Carrier. Grief engraved lines around his eyes and mouth. Shadow knew his thoughts dwelled beyond the fire. She reached out and touched his arm. Stone Carrier's head jerked a bit. His eyes came back into focus, looking at her. His lower lip trembled. He bit down on it. He managed the box on his own.

Munching on a rabbit leg, Shadow observed Stone Carrier eating. His face looked less drawn, more relaxed. But Shadow doubted that the sadness would ever leave his eyes.

Stone Carrier caught her watching him. He smiled. "It is delicious. Is there more?"

"Yes, yes." Shadow poured more broth into the box. She realized that Stone Carrier was seeing the cooking basket for the first time. Fear rose in her throat. The finely crafted basket was not made for cooking. With pine pitch covering the inside, it was useless for anything else now. Shadow held her breath and kept her eyes lowered. Now, his wrath would come for destroying the basket and using the stone box for drinking.

Stone Carrier finished his broth and set the box down. His eyelids looked heavy. He leaned his head back against the rocky wall. "Your mother has taught you well. She would be proud."

Shadow's cheeks flamed at the thought of what Mother would think if she knew *all* the dictates Shadow had defied.

"*Every woman must decide where she will stand, what battles she must fight, and what rules she must break to survive . . .*" Mother's words breathed in Shadow's mind.

Homesickness crashed down around her. She longed for Mother's loving arms, words of comfort, and unconditional love. Shadow fought back her tears. Unless she won the battle against the demon, she would never hug her mother again.

17

SHADOW INVENTED the perfect walking stick in her mind's eye. It had a wide fork that Stone Carrier could slip under his right arm for support and balance. Since the fingers on his right hand were unhurt, he could grip the stick despite the splint on that arm. Padding the fork with the rabbit pelts would make the fork tolerable. Stone Carrier had to manage with the walking stick just long enough to get off the demon's mountain. Once they were out of the its territory, Shadow planned on finding a safe place to stay until Stone Carrier was more fit to travel.

The mountainside loomed steeper, rockier—impassable in Shadow's mind as she examined Stone Carrier's ankle. Now black and blue, the bloated ankle was tender to the gentlest touch. Even if she found the perfect walking stick, she had doubts that Stone Carrier could even use it with his ankle in such bad condition. Worry drilled Shadow's mind during the night.

Finding a suitable walking stick occupied much of Shadow's effort the next two days. The first day, she searched the rubble of the rock slide. None of the branches trapped in the earth-flood suited her needs. Her search continued on her way to get water. She returned with a full canteen, another snared rabbit, some flavoring plants, an armful of firewood, and a heavy feeling of discouragement.

Stone Carrier ate the fresh stew without question. He commented on its flavor. "My cooking is so terrible that Sun refused to eat it." Stone Carrier's eyes glazed over with tears, but his lips formed a slight smile. "Two seasons ago, Sun insisted on cooking while we traveled."

A breath-stealing tightness gripped Shadow's throat. Two seasons ago, Sun's sudden interest in the mundane chore of preparing food had surprised her also.

"You, cook?" Her rebuff to Sun deluged Shadow's memory with vivid images and feelings of that day so long ago. "Men do not cook. Cooking is women's work."

Sun had placed his hands on his skinny hips. "I want to learn."

"If Stone Carrier finds out that you are doing women's work, he will—"

"Are you going to teach me, or am I going to have to ask Spring Breeze?" Sun's eyes had glared with determination.

"Sun could cook almost as well as you do." Stone Carrier's voice fragmented Shadow's memory.

Bittersweet sorrow consumed Shadow. Her tears stung.

The next day, her first snare was empty. The second snare proved barren also. "I will just keep going this way," she decided. "I can gather nuts and plants while watching for a stick."

The responsibility of providing food bore heavy on her shoulders. She began to understand the endless responsibility men carried. Even in lean times, her stomach had never suffered, thanks to Stone Carrier. Cooking seemed trivial to the task of obtaining the food. The tediously hard chore of grinding corn seemed like a privilege now.

"I wish I had a handful or two of corn *to grind*." Shadow knew that this wish was beyond her power to make come true.

"Please. Help me find a way to feed my father." The cool breeze combing the trees whisked her prayer away.

Shadow marked her path as she ranged farther into unknown territory. She gathered a few wilted, edible greens and found a shower of piñon nuts. Squirreling the nuts away in her bag, her stomach twisted. Her harvest would help ease their hunger, but not satisfy their bodies' need for strength-giving meat.

"It should not be so hard to find a simple walking stick," Shadow stated in a loud voice. Her frustration level lowered as her hunger increased. "I just need a long, forked stick strong enough to support Stone Carrier."

Her stomach rumbled.

Checking the sun, Shadow realized how late it was. "Stone Carrier will be hungry." Responsibility pressed heavier on her shoulders.

Ready to trek back, something within her refused to surrender to hunger and failure.

The whispering of the grass urged her onward, "Just a few steps more."

More than a few steps later, something hiding in a patch of dense, yellowing grass stubbed her toe. She saw the rounded tip of a bone buried deep in the grass. Shadow kicked the sun-bleached bone. It tumbled and bounced. Her toe smarted, and her anger ignited.

"You stupid thing." Shadow bent to snatch the bone. Something long, brown, and round lurking in the grass startled her. "A snake!"

Shadow staggered backward, expecting the thing to strike, coil, or slither away.

It did not move.

Shadow crept forward.

The object held perfectly still.

Pushing the grass aside, Shadow caught her breath. Her mind reeled. It was a spear. Pulling it up, she saw that it was just a spear shaft. A weathered, leather thong clung to the thin end of the shaft where it had once secured a spearhead. The thong had been gnawed, and it crumbled into pieces as Shadow touched it.

Clumps of dirt clung to the three-inch-round, wood pole. Prying the dirt off, Shadow shook her head in disbelief. Obsidian spearheads were routinely replaced on shafts, but the spear shafts were another matter. Great effort, skill, and time were expended creating such a fine shaft as this one. Men valued a spear shaft as much as they did their lives, which often depended on the strength and sureness of their spear.

"How did you get here?" Shadow ran her fingers up and down the wood. It stood taller than she. A deep crack, the length of Shadow's forearm, ran down the tapered end. Teeth marks mangled each side of the crack. The rest of the shaft felt true.

ROBERTS

RINEHART

ROBERTS RINEHART PUBLISHERS

PO BOX 666, Niwot, Colorado 80544-0666

TEL 303.530.4400   FAX 303.530.4488   rhinobooks@aol.com

To receive a free catalog of ROBERTS RINEHART books and audiotapes, please return this card. Indicate your interests by checking below:

☐ Art & Photography
☐ Children
☐ Young Adult
☐ History
☐ Fiction

☐ Irish Nonfiction
   (politics, culture, history)
☐ Natural History/Nature
☐ American West
☐ Travel

Name ....

Address ....

City .... State .... Zip ....

Title of this book: ....

Where purchased: ....

Comments: ....

ROBERTS
RINEHART

ROBERTS RINEHART PUBLISHERS

PO BOX 666
NIWOT CO 80544-0666

Place
Postage
Here

Scanning the area, Shadow spied other old bones concealed in the tall grass. Her mind clicked, piecing the information together. The vision of a deer or antelope fleeing for its life flashed in her mind. Red blood streamed from where the spearhead penetrated deep into the animal's shoulder. The spear's long shaft bobbed with each running stride. The keen projectile gashed deeper with each leap and bound.

More often than not, hunters tracked a wounded animal because they were not willing to lose their spears or their dignity. Old men and young recounted just such chases with great detail and pride. Few admitted defeat.

Shadow wondered why the hunter did not follow this animal. Her scalp tightened. Perhaps the hunter had become the hunted. This could be the demon's hunting ground. The possibility set her heart racing and her legs sprinting.

With her free hand, Shadow managed to find the Stone of Courage in her waist pouch. Shadow slowed to a jog. The spear shaft gave her a strange sense of balance while the stone in her hand endowed boldness.

Her pace became a fast walk as Shadow neared the serenity of the spring. Possibilities clicked in her mind. With yucca cordage, she could attach a forked branch to the shaft to make a walking stick. She leaned on the shaft to test its strength.

A new line of thinking volleyed in her mind. With some work, the shaft could return to its designated duty, hunting.

Hunting.

The muscles in her jaw tightened.

Splashing cold spring water on her face left her body covered with flesh-bumps. Shadow rinsed her face repeatedly. It still felt grimy—dirty with guilt from even thinking about making a weapon.

The spear shaft leaned against a rock nearby. She sat on her heels and stared at it.

"I am being silly," Shadow announced. "I have already hunted, taken rabbits in my snares. The earth did not break in half."

Shadow leaned toward the shaft. "I prayed for a way to feed Father. This is the answer."

Standing, Shadow lifted the shaft to ear level and balanced it. She thrust it back and forth in a throwing motion. With an awkward heave, she released it. The shaft hung in the air for a breath, then clattered to the ground, ten feet from her.

Her second throw was worse, and the third no better. "So much for feeding anyone with my mighty spear."

Mustering her bag and canteen, Shadow deserted the shaft where it landed. "The shaft is worthless if I cannot throw it. Besides, I would have to flake spear points."

More wasted time, more dictates defied.

No, what she really needed was a good walking stick. With a walking stick they could leave this place and go home. Safe at home, she had no need for a spear.

Still—

The thought of the village's reaction to her coming home carrying a spear filled her mind. Shadow walked on, visualizing the astonished villagers' faces as she marched into the plaza toting *her mighty* spear. The imagined details played before her. The men's faces flexed in anger. The women blushed but reached out to touch the magnificent buck she dragged behind her. Pride swelled Shadow's heart. She thrust back her shoulders, tilted her head high. Grace and agility marked her firm stride as she started up the demon's mountain, her mind lost in imaginary glory.

The demon's long, high wail slashed through Shadow's fantasy.

Shadow's knees turned to grass. Every hair on her shaking body bristled in fear.

Snarling crusted the air from the direction of the shelter.

Shadow bolted up. The demon's voice grew louder with each step. Her hand sought her knife.

Amusement rang in the demon's voice.

Clutching the knife, Shadow felt her foolishness. The knife was worthless, nothing but a small pebble.

88   Anger propelled Shadow. How dare the demon mock her.

Or was the demon delighting because it had somehow finally gotten to Stone Carrier?

Her legs pumped harder. Breathless fire charred her lungs. Dread stained her anger scarlet. "You cannot have my father!"

The demon wailed with delight.

18

SHADOW'S LOUD THREATS vaulted into battle cries as she blazed toward the shelter. "You cannot have my father. I will fight you. Fight you with everything in my body!"

Whether the demon believed her declaration or mocked it, Shadow did not know. The pandemonium of her rage choked her ears. Scalding determination surged her onward. "You will have to kill us both."

She burst up the incline to the shelter. Her lungs bellowed, and her knife swung.

The wood and rock wall stood untouched. Shadow jolted. She wheeled around, her knife daring even the smallest ant to move.

"Stone Carrier." Shadow tore rocks from the wall. "Are you all right?"

A groan came from within the shelter.

Bright light beamed out from the widening gap in the shelter's wall. Shadow thrust her head in. At the back of the shelter, Stone Carrier trembled, panic bulging his eyes. The leaping fire licked the low roof. "There is no more firewood. Get more wood to feed the fire."

Shadow pitched down another rock and twisted her head into the narrow opening. "You are safe." She strained to calm her voice as she widened the gap. "The demon is gone."

"No. It is still out there watching, waiting."

She squirmed into the shelter. The fire sprang at her as she scrunched past to Stone Carrier. "It cannot get us here." She wrapped her arms around him and held him tight. "I will not let it."

"We must keep the fire going." Stone Carrier's voice and body quivered. "Fire. All things living and dead respect fire; we must keep the fire roaring."

The intense heat made breathing difficult. The fire sucked

all the air from Shadow's lungs and made her head spin. Stone Carrier clung to her. Fear, mingled with sweat, soaked his body. His eyebrows were singed off. His finger-splints dug into her arms.

Shadow wiggled free.

"We will keep the fire going; but not so high." Sweat poured into her eyes. She realized Stone Carrier would have started burning the limbs and branches that supported the barricade if she had not returned. Terror garbled his logic.

Yet, she would have done the same thing if trapped here with only the fire for defense.

She needed cool air to steady her frenzied heart and clear her dizzy head. "The canteen and gathering bag are still outside. I will get them. You need water." Shadow edged past the fire.

"Daughter," Stone Carrier's voice was as intense as the fire. "Be careful."

Daughter!

Joy rang in Shadow's heart.

Outside, Shadow gulped air. Her mind sharpened.

Daughter. Stone Carrier claimed her as his daughter.

She grappled for her bag. A monstrous track glared up at her. A second print indented the dirt close by. Shadow's skin crawled at the sight.

"Four toe pads on the top, one heel pad. It is a huge dog or coyote's print. No, a dog's claw digs little slash-marks above each toe pad." She traced a print with her finger. "This heel pad is broader, flatter, and too round on the bottom to be a coyote's."

Shadow bit her lip in concentration, trying to connect the tracks before her with the demon's wailing cries and high-pitched screams. Terror riddled her mind. "A mountain lion."

She glared at the tracks not wanting to accept the possibility, yet knowing her assumption was correct. There was no more feared enemy than the huge mountain cats that ran with the speed of lightning and had the power of thunder and the cunning of a fox. Their long claws ripped life from deer, antelope, or man. Their large amber eyes glowed as their keen   **91** teeth devoured their kill. They were known to feast on their kill for a time, then half-bury the carcass with dirt. Hours later, they would return to feed again.

Shadow eased her hands into one imprint. The track encased her outspread fingers with inches to spare. She visualized a huge, sleek, tan cat stalking back and forth, trying to find a way to reach Stone Carrier.

Her wall had kept the lion out. A major battle won.

She studied each print to gain more insight into her enemy. Something about their shallow depth and wide spacing nagged at her mind.

Shadow traced a second track and then another and rummaged through her memory for everything Sun had taught her about tracks. Facts tumbled around inside her mind. She sifted through each. None scratched the itch in her mind.

Darkness began to encase the mountain. Coldness bore into Shadow's bones. Homesickness racked her heart. If only she were at home, safe with Mother.

"Shadow," Stone Carrier's anxious voice catapulted out of the shelter. "Shadow!"

Taking one last cool breath, Shadow answered. "I am coming."

Terror had driven both of their hunger away. Shadow steeped greens in hot water along with herbs and a few nuts. Stone Carrier ate little, Shadow less.

"I found tracks outside." Shadow examined Stone Carrier's ankle. The bruising-color was still intense, and the swelling still very evident.

"I think it is from a mountain lion." Shadow stated.

Stone Carrier's eyes sharpened on her. His lips pulled tight. One eyebrow arched up. He parted his mouth, then clamped it closed. After a deep breath and a moment of thought, he nodded.

"The tracks look odd," Shadow sat back. "But I am not sure why."

"It is not *just* a mountain lion. It is a demon cat, a fiend no one dares face."

Shadow stared straight at her father. "You did. Sun did." Stone Carrier's shoulders slumped, and he shut his eyes.

Curled under the rabbit-skin blanket next to Stone Carrier, Shadow fought sleep. She searched for answers to the worries tormenting her weary mind. Shadow tried to analyze what was strange about the cat's tracks and came up with nothing. She had never heard a mountain lion before, yet she knew that there was something strange about this one's cries and snarls. Father had said it was not just a mountain lion. Shadow did not doubt this for a minute, but she was somehow relieved to know what she was facing. At least the demon had a shape, a body, a face now.

Her mind went on to examine the problem of the walking stick—where to find one, or if Stone Carrier could even use one to get down the steep mountainside. She knew that it would take more than just a walking stick to battle the demon lion.

Shadow began concentrating on how to repair the spear shaft and went on to think about knapping suitable spear points. She was certain she could make points. But it would take practice, a lot of practice, until she could kill something with the spear at close range—demon-close.

Shadow flinched and thrust the thought aside.

He called me, "daughter."

Her eyelids closed. Peace beat within her heart, and sleep cloaked her.

When Shadow's eyes opened again, the woven-wood barricade was the first thing she saw. Dim daylight eked through the cracks between the branches, boughs, and outside rocks. Curled up next to Stone Carrier, she felt too warm and secure to move. Her eyes meandered along the wood lines of the barricade.

"It is a good barricade. Even Sun could not have made it tighter or firmer." Shadow's thoughts paused as her eyes reached an intersection in the wood web. The fork of one branch interlocked with a larger limb. It had been difficult to wedge the two so tight, but the fork had finally supported the burden of the limb.

Shadow sprang up, pulling the shared rabbit blanket off of Stone Carrier. He stirred.

"What is it?" Stone Carrier swayed up on one arm. "The demon?"

The forked branch was wedged solid near the top of the barricade. She tugged on it gently and leaned back. "I found your walking stick. I have looked at it every day but did not see it. The trick is getting it out without crumbling the entire wall." She twisted the branch at different angles. The wood structure popped and groaned.

"Balance and support."

Shadow faced her father. "What?"

Stone Carrier smiled. "Everything in life must have balance and support to stand."

It took little time for Shadow to find a substitute limb for the forked branch. It took longer wedging it beside the forked branch to ease its burden. After a gentle-firm pull, the forked branch slipped into Shadow's eager hands.

"Your balance." Shadow held the walking stick out. "And your support."

The edge of her knife dulled quickly sawing the stick to make it the right length for Stone Carrier. "I will just make another knife," she thought, confident in her ability.

Minutes later, Shadow supported Stone Carrier's weight and hoisted him. "Watch your head."

Stone Carrier gripped her arm and rolled his shoulders. He used the walking stick for balance as he heaved himself up. His head smacked the top of the hollow. He bent lower but still managed to slip the fork under his arm. Sweat pebbled his forehead. "It feels about right, but . . . "

"It is hard to tell when not standing up straight," Shadow interrupted. She bit her lip. Stone Carrier hated interruptions.

He nodded and slumped back down.

"You are still weak." Shadow tucked the blanket around him. She knew that his ankle was still very painful. His ribs must revolt against every jostle and tug, yet he did not complain.

"Rest while I go for water."

Worry streaked Stone Carrier's face.

Shadow promised, "I will be careful."

Outside, the day was dim and cool. Leaden clouds camouflaged the sky.

"Thank you for providing the walking stick for my father," Shadow prayed as she ran. "Please help me protect him. Give me the courage to do what must be done."

Her feet could not carry her fast enough.

The spear waited for her.

THE SPEAR SHAFT TWISTED, wobbled, and slumped to the ground. Shadow kneaded her knotted arm. After hundreds of launches in the past day and a half, her muscles still complained at each hurl. Her distance was improving, her aim was off, and her frustration mounting. She was wasting time—time she did not have. Too much time had already been spent just repairing the spear.

In order to shorten the shaft, Shadow had to flake a saw-type tool. Although the job had sharpened her knapping ability, it had taken too long. A drift of flakes on the ground, her many failures, told of her persistence. Or her stubbornness.

Cutting the shaft off below the crack had taken less time and was time well spent. The shortened shaft responded to her efforts with less resistance.

Shadow scanned the area around her. She jogged to her spear, watching over her shoulder. Mountain lions preferred attacking from the rear, biting the necks of their victims whose time had run out.

Her time was running out, too.

Yesterday, fresh mountain lion tracks encircled the shelter's entrance. This morning, a trail of tracks led from the spring. The cat had stalked her. She had felt its deadly presence slinking behind her. As always, the cat had kept out of sight.

As she hurled her spear, Shadow wondered how soon the demon would tire of its game of cat and mouse.

Too soon, she was sure.

"Hand me your walking stick." The gap in the barrier was wide enough to accommodate Stone Carrier. Shadow stood on the outside, looking in.

Stone Carrier leaned against the inside framework. He

maneuvered the stickthrough the opening, and Shadow pulled him into the daylight. Pain tensed his face, sweat dripped from his forehead, and he slumped to the ground. His eyes darted around.

Shadow knelt beside him. "Which bothers you the worse, your ankle or ribs?"

"My fear. Help me up."

Shadow slid the fork of the stick under Stone Carrier's arm. "Go slow and easy."

Stone Carrier cocked an eyebrow. "Like my daughter?"

He adjusted the padded fork under his arm. "The soft rabbit pelts feel better than the rough branch. Thank you."

A warm blush streamed up Shadow's neck to her face.

Stone Carrier's splinted arm rested against the stick, and his good fingers encircled it. His left hand's mangled fingers hung helpless on the opposite side.

"If only he had one workable hand and arm," Shadow thought.

He hobbled forward.

Shadow cringed at the sight of his ankle as it skimmed the ground. It was laughable to even think that Stone Carrier could climb down the mountainside. Then there were the endless miles home. Discouragement flooded Shadow. They would never make it.

After two steps, Stone Carrier paused, wiping the sweat from his eyes. "One step, just one step at a time. Those are my father's words. His orders when I tangled my running feet. 'One step at a time,' he scolded every time I failed."

"But you never fail," Shadow blurted out.

"In my father's eyes, I always failed. He was blind to everything except perfection, and I have never been perfect." Stone Carrier heaved forward on his stick, this time dangling his ankle off the ground.

"One step at a time." He shuffled ahead without Shadow's help. After five painful hobbles, he angled around. Leaning on his stick, pain chiseled his smile. "Not one perfect step, only distance. Only needed distance."

Stone Carrier took ten steps forward, veered, and retraced **97** them. He rested a handful of minutes, then struggled back and forth again. Time after time. Finally, he toppled beside Shadow.

Rolling yucca fibers on her thigh, Shadow regarded Stone Carrier. She counted each rib as his chest heaved. With eyes closed, his long, dark lashes stood out against his skin. His arms and legs were emaciated, what little muscled remained, strained. She had tried to stop him long ago, but he ignored her requests, his stubbornness showing through.

Shadow asked, "Will you go back in and rest now?"

Stone Carrier agreed, almost too tired to crawl back into the shelter.

"I will be right outside, working."

"The demon?" Stone Carrier slumped just inside in the shelter.

Tucking the blanket around him, Shadow answered, "I will rock-up the wall again and will hurry back in if the demon so much as burps." Her voice sounded braver than she felt.

"Work in here." Stone Carrier mumbled. His eyes shut, and sleep snatched him away.

Even with Stone Carrier asleep, Shadow did not dare work within his view. She could not risk his anger and rejection. His acceptance was too new, too delicate, too precious.

Shadow crawled out and rocked up the barricade, leaving only a small hole. Checking around her, she scurried to the nearest tree and wrangled the spear shaft from its hiding place among the branches.

After starting a small fire, Shadow fetched hunks of obsidian. Her fingers tingled with anxiety. Her mind pricked with guilt. The gods on the sacred Father Mountain were surly debating how to show their anger.

Shadow turned a chunk of stone in her hand. Her mother's words suddenly sprang to her uneasy mind.

"Life is too precious to cast off in the name of custom."

The meaning of the words rang true in her mind. "I understand Mother," Shadow whispered. "I just hope the gods agree."

Her first attempt at flaking a spear point ended with the

first strike. Her hammer stone smacked the edge of the obsidian too close. The resulting flake was too thin.

She started again. A thicker flake tumbled off into her hand. Shadow studied the flake and matched it with the spear point in her mind's eye. "No," she groaned, casting the flake aside.

Knapping the initial flake took six attempts. Finally, she held a flake that appeared workable. "It needs to be thinned a bit here." Shadow used a thinner stone to flake it. Small, sharp pieces fell off with each blow.

Shadow turned the glistening stone in her hand. She pressed it to the tip of her shaft. "It will fit."

Chipping the stone into a triangular shape took all her skill and patience. The stone slowly took on the appearance of a point. Pressing the antler carefully against the edge of the stone, Shadow honed a fine tip. On the alternate side of the point, she repeated the process, sharpening the point to a flesh-splitting keenness.

She took a deep breath. It was a good point. Better than she had ever dreamed of. Perhaps the gods were on her side.

The point needed grooves notched into each side of its base. Fresh sinew would wrap around and through the grooves to attach the point to the spear.

"The tip of an antler might work best for the notching." Shadow steadied her hand. With the first notch completed, she felt confident. "The second notch will be easier, now that I know how. Good." She scrutinized her last notch. "Not deep enough, just one more flake will fix that."

The force of her antler split through the stone to the opposite notch. The base of the spear point fell to the ground.

"No!" Frustration and disappointment swept over Shadow. Anger tagged close behind.

Shadow began the time-consuming, patience-eroding, life-saving process again.

Rabbit-flavored smoke curled around the small fire built outside of the shelter. Shadow rotated the spit. The fire sizzled with dripping fat. She wondered if Stone Carrier's stomach was ready for the strength-giving meat. Not having to make broth meant time saved.

Time was precious.

Time had flown as she had struggled to make a spear point. Time vanished while adjusting and tethering the point firmly to the shaft with rabbit sinew. She was doubly grateful to the rabbit. Time dashed as she waited for the rabbit to roast. Shadow flaked another point, racing time. She lost. Too much time taken.

She wondered what time schedule the demon kept. All it seemed to do was taunt and torment her. It was most likely spying on her at this minute.

Leaping up, Shadow gripped her spear. Her eyes searched. Light shifted in and out of the trees. She lunged forward. The projectile slashed the dying day. Shadow slipped back and sprang forward, once again, her spear leading the way. Lurching, she drove and stabbed at her unseen foe.

"Grip your spear farther back. Be sure of your balance before you thrust."

Startled, Shadow pivoted.

Stone Carrier's skeletal face looked out from the crawl hole in the barrier.

20

SHADOW CLUTCHED THE SPEAR so tightly that the blood drained from her fingers. Her knees knocked. She pulled them tight and braced for Stone Carrier's blistering anger.

"Square your shoulders." Stone Carrier's voice sounded eerie echoing from within the shelter.

Shadow's shoulders went back. She could not swallow or breathe.

"Bring your left foot forward. Now, bend the knees a bit. Not so much. Put those shoulders back more. Use their power to guide your thrust. Fix your sight on your target. Lunge and thrust."

Tingling tightness spread across Shadow's shoulder blades and up her neck. The hair on her scalp tightened. This could not be happening. It was just another of her too-real dreams.

Stone Carrier's voiced instructed, "Spear tip up. Eyes on your target. Lunge and thrust."

Shadow concentrated. She thrust forward, following her spear into the air.

"Good." Stone Carrier's voice sounded pleased. "Help me out of here. While you practice with your spear, I will work with my stick."

In a fearful trance, Shadow hurried to the barricade and began widening the crawl hole. The rocks in her hands felt real. Stone Carrier's drawn face, peering out of opening, was more than real.

His mouth was pulled straight, but his eyes were laughing at her.

This was all a strange and twisted nightmare. It just had to be. Shadow nabbed another stone. It slipped and rolled. Pain exploded in her fingers! Whirling around, Shadow clutched her fingers while shaking her hand.

"Are you all right?" Deep concern reflected in Stone Carrier's eyes—the same concern that Shadow had seen a thousand times burning in his eyes. Each and every time, the concern had been for Sun.

"You are improving."

Shadow shot back, "So are you, but you need to rest."

"I was going to suggest the same for you." Using his stick, Stone Carrier lowered himself to the ground. A groan of relief slipped from his lips.

Shadow followed, resting her spear across her lap.

"May I see your spear?" Somehow he balanced it with his splintered fingers.

Fear tiptoed along Shadow's spine as she watched him examining the shaft.

His eyebrows arched. "It has been shortened." He glanced at her, then back at the spear. "You?"

"Yes." The word burned Shadow's mouth. "Something had chewed the end and cracked it."

"You did well. This length suits your arm." Stone Carrier's thumb tested the spearhead's lashing and nodded. He probed the point.

Moisture washed her palms and dotted her forehead.

Stone Carrier took a deep breath and held it three, four, five heartbeats. His tensed face eased. "Sun did not teach you to flake stone."

Shadow's chin quivered. She managed to shake her head as tears smudged her vision. She needed to defend Sun, to say that he would never teach her such sacred things. Shadow tried to think of a way to explain that what little technical knowledge she possessed came from a lifetime of observing a master stone knapper, and that her limited skill was the product of trial and error. Mostly error. She wanted to vindicate Sun, take the rightful blame, but a tightening ache in her throat throttled her words.

"Wherever Sun went, his Shadow followed." Stone Carrier spoke more to himself than to her. "He taught you many things, but not flaking stone." His eyes brimmed. "Sun was a good teacher, and you a fast learner."

"He learned to cook faster than I did." Tears burned her face.

Stone Carrier smiled. "And you must learn to use the spear quicker than he did."

The spear point's tip broke after only two throws. Shadow tried to hide her anger by digging into her waist pouch. "I have another one."

"I get infuriated when my points break." Stone Carrier responded with surprising calmness. "Practice with the broken point. It will still add the needed weight and balance. Save your good point and switch it later."

It was close to dusk when they stopped working. Fatigue shook Stone Carrier's body. Pain engraved his face. Shadow's shoulders were numb from heaving and thrusting the spear. Getting Stone Carrier into the shelter took all of their strength.

"I must go for water before it grows darker." Shadow settled him down and fed the fire back to life.

"It can wait."

"There are only a few drops left, and my snares need . . ." She stopped herself.

Worry shimmered in Stone Carrier's eyes. "Then at least change spear points before you go."

Under his direction, the new point was lashed to the spear without time wasted.

Shadow found her first snare shredded. Fluffs of rabbit fur clung to the tattered fibers. Something had stolen her kill. She crouched closer. Her anger vaulted into fear. Fresh blood seeped into a huge cat print.

She yanked the canteen's stopper out with her teeth, unwilling to surrender the spear from her other hand. Her eyes scoured the trees, rocks, bushes, even the tall grass around the spring. Not lowering her eyes, she knelt. Icy water swallowed the canteen and her hand. The blurp of bubbles escaping the canteen's mouth glutted the tomb-quiet air. Shadow's scalp pulled tight. The birds and insects that always serenaded her were missing.

A stench infiltrated Shadow's nose. She gagged, fighting her empty stomach down.

The canteen felt full. Wrenching it and herself up, she replaced the stopper and jammed it in the gathering bag slung over her shoulder.

Behind her, the trees vibrated.

Shadow careened, her spear up. Dying daylight obscured visual details but heightened the sense of death lurking nearby.

She moved backward, trying to see her enemy, but saw nothing. Three, four, half a dozen steps later she veered around and sprinted away.

A contemptuous snarl curled the air behind her.

"Please, help me run faster," Shadow prayed over her thundering heart. She glanced back. A murky, shifting form silhouetted the trail behind her.

The bag banged against her aching side as she hurtled on. The air boiled in her scorched lungs. "Please, the shelter is just a—"

Hideous wailing echoed around and through Shadow. Her feet hitched together. She sprawled face-first, her breath knocked out of her. Cold water sloshed out of the canteen, soaking her.

The spear bounced ahead, leaving her behind. She crawled after it, trying to catch her breath.

Squeals of arrogant laughter whipped the air. "Silly child. How I enjoyed watching you fail."

Shadow groped for the spear in the gathering darkness. Grasping it, she gritted her teeth. Anger restored her breath. "I will not fail!" she screamed, getting to her feet.

Stone Carrier somehow managed to help pull her and the spear through the crawl hole. Gasping for air, she heaved the rocks into the opening, one after another. With each rock, victory clamored in her heart.

"I won," she declared, picking up the last stone. "I won this battle." She peered out the fist-sized opening.

Three feet from the wall, two huge amber eyes blazed eerily against the darkness. The cat snarled. Its hate-filled eyes blinked, then widened. Its wail seemed to say, "The game is just beginning!"

Shadow thrust the final stone into its place in the wall.

Sʜᴀᴅᴏᴡ ꜱʟᴜᴍᴘᴇᴅ against the barricade and clamped her eyes shut. She waited for her pounding heart to burst. Terror racked her body in ice cold, wet waves.

"The game is just beginning." The mountain lion's threat hammered her mind and her soul.

Shadow could not, would not play the game any longer. She was too cold, too weary, too worn down. Her courage stretched breath-thin, too fragile to struggle any longer. She just wanted to be at Sun's side, doing whatever spirits did on sacred Father Mountain.

"Daughter."

Stone Carrier's wood-bound fingers touched her arm. The warmth of the rabbit-skinblanket enfolded her. The emotional dam that held her feelings in check for so long crumbled. She began sobbing.

Stone Carrier pulled her against his chest. "Shadow, my brave daughter."

He let her cry out her frustration, her grief, her homesickness, her fear, and finally, herself.

When she opened her eyes, embers glowed in the fire pit. Stone Carrier's head rested against her head in sleep. The spear lay inches from both of them.

Shadow wiped the sleep and dried tears from her eyes. "The spear point is broken."

Stone Carrier jerked up. Shadow slipped from his arms.

"You will make another one." Stone Carrier's voice slurred with sleep.

"There is no time. We must leave now, before the mountain lion comes back." Shadow stashed her belongings into the gathering bag.

Stone Carrier stopped her. "The cat sees in the dark. We do not."

"Then we must leave the instant we can see an inch in

front of our noses." Shadow shook the canteen. It felt only half full. Her damp skirt and top reminded her why. They would have to find water on the way back to the village.

The village.

Her back bent, and her shoulders slumped. Shadow shook her head. The lion would never let them leave the mountain alive.

An image tickled her fatigued mind.

Laughter bubbled in her chest. It boiled up her throat and out of her mouth. Her father's eyes widened.

Shadow tired to stop laughing, but could not. A hilarious fantasy played in her mind of what they must look like to the lion. A wirey girl who quaked like leaves on an aspen tree as she toted a giant spear shaft with no point. A muscle-withered man with a wooden arm and mangled fingers, hopped along on a rabbit-covered stick, trying to escape down the mountain.

It was all useless, so useless that it was funny. There was no way they could escape the demon.

"Shadow."

She bit her tongue till she tasted blood. Still the morbid humor of the situation plagued her. "I cannot stop thinking about how foolish we seem to the mountain lion."

"Courage is never foolish." Stone Carrier was rigid. "Courage is the only thing that the demon fears."

Courage.

"Women must be stronger and more courageous to survive." Mother's words and swollen face leapt into Shadow's mind. Mother needed her. Surely, her sister had been born by now. She was sure Mother's courage sustained her during childbirth, and she prayed that her baby sister had the strength and courage to live also. Shadow's arm's ached to hug Mother and cradle her unknown sister.

"We must go home," Shadow said in a low, strong voice. "Mother and my new sister need me."

Surprise flashed in Stone Carrier's face. "A sister?" A smile twitched his lips. "Yes, she will need you to teach her many things."

"I must flake a new spear—" Shadow swallowed the rest of her word. Her heart sank with an uttered groan. She had no more obsidian.

"Daughter?"

"I have no obsi—" she began, suddenly taking notice of the rock barricade. "There must be a large piece of obsidian among all those stones I hauled!" Shadow rummaged deep into the wood web to see the rocks on the other side. The light was too dim. She threw a handful of dry pine needles into the fire. Shadow pushed aside a familiar branch and slid her hammer stone and antler pieces from their hiding place. She searched each stone from the top to the bottom of the barricade.

"Nothing." Shadow sat back on her heels, thinking. "My knife! I can flake it into a spear point." Her knife was at the top of her pouch.

Stone Carrier leaned forward. "It is not large enough."

Frustration and fear stabbed at her. She had no choice but to go outside to find a suitable core of obsidian. Shadow tried to shove her knife back into the pouch. Her kicking ball blocked the pouch's opening. Pulling the ball out, Shadow threw it to the ground. It rolled up against Stone Carrier's foot.

He shook his head. "Other than flaking stone, was there anything that Sun did not share with you?"

"The wisdom of always having obsidian." Now, something else blocked the opening of her waist pouch. Shadow yanked on the knotted wad of cordage. Something was tangled in it. She plucked at it, unsnarling the cord. Warmth and strength flowed into her fingers.

"The Stone of Courage." Shadow freed the tear-shaped obsidian and held it up. In the fire's light, the red figure within the stone seem to reach outward to her.

Visions of a tear-shaped spearhead flared in Shadow's head. She turned the stone over, touched its tip, and honed it in her mind. She traced along the stone's smooth edges and felt the potential keenness. The stone's round bottom was wide enough to accommodate notches.

Shadow glanced at her father. His expert stone knapper's eyes saw what she envisioned: a spear point.

"Hold the tip of the antler closer to the edge," Stone Carrier instructed. "Press gently, test the stone's strength first."

Shadow did and prayed silently, "Please guide my hands."

With her first pressure strike, the stone seemed to come alive in her hands. It directed the antler where to chip, flake, and sharpen. It whispered courage and strength to Shadow's heart.

Shadow handed the finished spear point to Stone Carrier. He examined it. "I could not do better. Your hands listened to your heart."

"No," Shadow said, taking the stone back. She held it up. The figure's head rested just below the keen point. "They listened to the spirit of the stone."

Nothing breathed on the mountain, including Shadow. She held her breath, straining to see the uneven ground beneath her feet in the gray darkness just before the morning's first light. It was easier to let her toes feel the way. Shadow felt Stone Carrier at her shoulder.

If only they could go the shortest way, straight down the mountainside on her well-worn path. They could be off the mountain and long gone before the first rays of sun warmed the morning air.

Instead, they zigzagged back and forth, inching down the steep contour of the mountain. Stone Carrier struggled to keep his walking stick and legs under him.

Shadow used the spear to keep her balance. How far had they gone?

"Not far enough," Shadow answered herself. She could see a few feet ahead and behind now. She glanced over her shoulder. Stone Carrier's face twisted in pain with each step. Meeting her eyes, he nodded, and pointed onward with his chin.

She cut back across the side of the incline. Her foot slipped. She sank the bottom of the spear shaft into the **109** ground to stop her fall. The spearhead stood just inches from her face. In the growing light, Shadow made out the woman's figure with her head held high and shoulders squared, her red garment shifting and swaying.

The hair on Shadow's neck prickled. She glanced around and saw nothing but eerie shadows cast by the trees and bushes.

Stone Carrier panted just behind her. He must have sensed the mountain lion near, but his face reflected only pain.

Shadow pushed on, her spear ready, her heart racing.

Tinges of peachy-pink decorated the sky to the east. Her eyes shot everywhere—in front, to the side, to the back of her. Shadow did not see the cat. She felt it.

Sweat drenched Stone Carrier's face, chest, and arms despite the cold air. His skin looked ashen. Shadow stopped and waited for him to pull closer. "I need to rest," she whispered.

He nodded and leaned heavily on his stick, trying to catch his breath.

Shadow's eyes searched the mountainside as her hands groped for the canteen in the gathering bag. Pulling it out, she passed it to her father.

She heard him gulp once. The canteen was pressed back to her. It went back into the bag. Still nothing moved around them. Shadow was not fooled; she knew the cat was close.

Nothing on earth moved so silently. Why, even the wind rustled the leaves and grass. No physical thing could be so totally invisible. Father was correct. The lion was not just a mere cat.

She looked at her father. Her heart ached. The short distance had taken much from him, and he did not have much more to give. Touching his shoulder, she whispered, "We are almost to the tree line. It is not as steep there as it is here."

Stone Carrier nodded.

The cat could hide even more easily in the trees, Shadow realized. A frigid breeze stabbed her back. She reeled around. The cat's stench filled her nose.

The tall trees threw twisted shadows on the mountain's side. Shadow paused again. Stone Carrier refused water. "We must keep going."

The floor of pine needles and leaves swallowed the tip of Stone Carrier's walking stick. Their pace slowed. Shadow slipped her shoulder under Stone Carrier's left arm. "Lean on me." Their pace picked up.

A snarl came from behind them. An instant later, a long, high wail sounded to their left.

Shadow ducked out from under Stone Carrier's arm, spear raised.

The mountain lion howled from just ahead of them. Shadow pivoted.

Mocking shrills peeled from behind her.

"Nothing moves that fast," Shadow said between gritted teeth.

Stone Carrier hobbled forward. "The demon does." He lost his footing and went down.

The cat laughed in delight.

"Leave me," Stone Carrier ordered as Shadow bent down to him.

She tugged his splintered arm over her shoulder and heaved. "We are almost down now. Once we are off its mountain, it will leave us alone."

Stone Carrier wrenched backward. "Go without me."

"The more you resist getting to your feet, the more you are going to hurt your ribs." Shadow strained under his weight.

Stone Carrier heaved upward and onto the walking stick. "You are as stubborn as—"

"As my father." Shadow propelled him on.

Growling—both the demon's and Stone Carrier's— rippled the air.

Shadow's heart drummed. The cat's voice drew closer. It screeched from every direction and swirled around Shadow and Stone Carrier like a breath-sucking vapor.

Shadow's hand cramped from gripping the spear so tightly. Her shoulders ached under Stone Carrier's weight. Her legs felt like boulders. She forced her mind to think, to plan, to see any strategies. Nothing surfaced but raw determination and the will to live.

"The game is coming to an end, silly child," The cat snarled. "Your end."

The ground tapered and leveled out a mere twenty steps ahead. Brightened by hope, Shadow became reenergized.

"We are almost off the mountain." Somehow, the magic line between life and death encircled the foot of Demon's Mountain.

Stone Carrier whispered, "Please, give me strength."

Hearing her father's prayer, Shadow added her pleas. "Give us courage."

Stone Carrier tripped. Shadow held him up.

Together, they stumbled over the perimeter of the mountain, the line of life and death.

Shadow shrieked, "We did it. We won!"

The mountain lion answered with an angry bawl.

"Keep going," Stone Carrier's voice came in between pants and stabs of pain. "Do not stop."

The pleasure of triumph flooded Shadow until she saw in her father the cost of her personal victory. Fear was the only color in his bloodless face. Pain contorted every inch of his body. Death shrouded his drooping shoulders.

She pressed on. "There is a place where we can rest. It is not far."

But even the lizard rock seemed too far for Stone Carrier to go.

22

THE LIZARD ROCK STOOD its stoic watch. Its stone head lifted five feet above the ground. Its huge hind legs spread firmly below. The burrow under its large stomach offered safety.

Easing Stone Carrier down against the massive rock, Shadow's heart sank. In her memory, the entrance under the lizard's stone stomach was large enough for her to squeeze through easily.

"It is big enough for a girl, but not for a grown man," Shadow screamed at herself. How stupid of her.

Shadow fumbled for the canteen. "There is a chamber under the rock. It is where I found the Stone of Courage. You can rest there."

Stone Carrier eyed the small, dark opening. "Only a mole could fit in."

"I will make it bigger," Shadow replied.

She slipped the gathering bag from her shoulder. Tension twisted inside her. Stone Carrier could go no farther. They would be safe here only if she could make the opening wider. "Stay here. I will find something to dig with."

Clutching her spear, she scooted toward a growth of trees to the east. A broad piece of wood would work. She picked up a half-rotted log, then threw it down. Not sturdy enough. Shadow hurried on, trying to remember whether the tunnel was the length of one body or two. It did not matter. She would get Stone Carrier in and block up the entrance with stones as she had on the mountain. Stone Carrier could rest. In a few hours they would go on.

The mountain lion's shrill laughter pierced her heart. Shadow sped back through the trees toward where she had left Stone Carrier.

Shadow saw the massive cat toying with Stone Carrier, trapped against the lizard rock two hundred steps beyond. The sleek, midnight-colored cat swiped its huge paws at Stone Carrier with mocking snarls. Stone Carrier blocked the cat's paws with the end of his walking stick.

Shadow realized that it was a mere game to the mountain lion. Its claws could shred the stick with one blow.

What was it waiting for? Shadow's mind worked in clear precision, faster than her legs moved.

Mountain lions were tan in color; this cat was black like the one in her vision.

"It is not just a mountain lion. It is a demon." Stone Carrier's words whirled in her mind.

The cat's uncanny speed, its undetected movements, the shallow depth of its tracks. It all added together, some way.

The giant cat had let her come and go off its mountain. Why had it let her live?

Why did it let her father live now?

"Courage is the only thing the demon fears." Again Stone Carrier's words sprang to mind.

Courage.

The fragmented pieces of the puzzles slipped into place in Shadow's mind.

Courage was the Spirit of Fear's greatest enemy.

Shadow's breath ripped through her chest as she screamed. "Father!"

The demon slowly turned its head. It seemed to leer with satisfaction.

She smelled death.

"Run!" Stone Carrier shouted. "Get away!"

The cat snarled with annoyance. It raised its huge paw. Hand-long claws glistened in the sun.

"No!" Shadow was still too far to use her spear. Sprinting, she ripped her waist pouch open and gripped her kicking ball. Pausing, she took aim and hurled it toward the cat.

The ball sailed through the air. Shadow followed ten breaths behind.

The hard ball completely passed through the cat's dark

body and bounced off the rock just inches above Stone Carrier's head.

In the same breath, the cat vanished in a puff of smoke and reappeared on top of the lizard rock. Shadow recognized the Spirit of Fear's eyes glaring at her as she drew closer.

The Spirit of Fear, disguised as the demon cat, screamed in rage and crouched to spring.

Shadow squared her shoulders, and lifted the tip of her spear.

The cat leaped into the air. Its powerful muscles rippled as it stretched itself down toward Shadow.

Shadow lunged upward with the spear, the Spirit of Courage surging in the spearhead.

In midair, the spear point thrust deep into the demon's exposed chest.

Shadow bounced backward and hit the ground. The Spirit of Fear's body writhed and twisted in the air above her. It snarled, bawled, and screamed, the spear point twisting deeper into its heart.

With a loud hiss, the Spirit of Fear vanished.

The form of a woman, the Spirit of Courage, instantly took its place. Her red dress swayed like evening clouds in the wind. Waist-long, dark hair swirled around her heart-shaped face. She swirled upward in graceful flutters, dips and whirls, celebrating their victory.

Shadow lifted herself up. "Thank you," she said, finding her voice.

The Spirit of Courage spun toward Shadow. Her smooth face radiated the beauty of the night. Her eyes shone with the strength of the day. Her voice sang with the whisper of the winds. "It is I who owe gratitude." She glided down. Her feet did not touch the ground, yet she looked Shadow in the eye.

"Your courage has set me free."

Shadow asked, "The demon, the Spirit of Fear, is it—"

"Is it dead? No. Fear will always live on to stalk, taunt, and kill one's spirit."

The Spirit of Courage extended her graceful hand. "But 115

your courage and strength have set me free after hundreds of years of being trapped within the stone. Now, I can walk beside all our sisters who need courage." She caressed Shadow's cheek with a touch as soft as a pleasant dream. Tears sparkled in her bright eyes. "I will share your courage with our sisters."

With a smile, the Spirit of Courage vanished.

MOVING LIKE PINE PITCH, Shadow and Stone Carrier took an entire day to reach a secluded forest-cove that Stone Carrier knew of. There, water sputtered from the ground, and rabbits ran in herds. Stone Carrier's and Shadow's stomachs were full enough to gain strength but empty enough to allow clear sight and humility.

They spent five days there, resting and learning. Stone Carrier taught Shadow to peel the pelt from a rabbit without using a knife. Shadow shared the art of rubbing herbs into the meat before roasting it. Stone Carrier nurtured Shadow's growing knapping skills and directed her spear throwing. She cared for his healing wounds.

It was a time of giving, taking, listening, sharing, grieving, and mending. A time for conceding apologies and granting forgiveness. Five days of growing stronger in body and heart.

Then came four long days of walking. While they slowly journeyed home, father and daughter swapped memories of Sun's escapades, good deeds, generosity, and love. Their tears swelled as their hearts twined together in sorrow.

As they spoke of Mother and the new sister, worry nagged Shadow that neither Mother nor the baby would be there to greet them. Many women and their babies died in childbirth. Shadow could not envision life without her mother.

She did not envy Stone Carrier's task of telling Mother of Sun's death. Shadow's own grief was a constant companion now, and she worried about how Mother would bear the loss.

The nearer they got to the village, the less heavily Stone Carrier leaned on his walking stick, and the heavier Shadow's worries weighed. She doubted that she could slip back into the narrow crack that the world had carved for her. That niche seemed so small, so impossible to breathe in now. How could she abandon her newly developed skills, trade her spear for a grinding stone?

Yet, she did not want the responsibility she had carried for so long. Shadow longed to run, laugh, and play as carefree as a child. She wished to hear the chatter and pleasantries of the village women while she worked beside them.

"Everything in life must have balance and support to stand." Stone Carrier's words repeated themselves in Shadow's mind.

Balance and support.

Support. Mother and Father were her supports. Their love would sustain her in what she chose to do. Shadow knew this with all her heart.

Balance. There had to be a balance between village life, customs, and expectations and her new found identity, freedom, and skills. But how she would find and maintain this equilibrium plagued Shadow's mind with every step toward the village.

Surely, other women faced the same quandary; fitting into society while still being themselves. Mother and old Child Bringer had inner peace and harmony, yet they did more than other women in the village with their healing skills. Shadow thought of the women in her village. There were others that seemed to have balanced their outstanding accomplishments in pottery, basketry, and other skills with what was expected of them. She would watch these special women and learn their secrets of balance, and she would ask Mother and Child Bringer for guidance in finding inner peace and harmony. They would share their insights with her and help her find a balance.

After much thought, Shadow realized that only *she* could find, establish, and maintain her balance and inner peace. It would be a daily quest requiring courage, strength, and patience. But somehow—some way, with the help of the Spirit of Courage—Shadow knew she had to achieve a balance between what she had learned, achieved, and become. There was no going back, just a delicate line to walk

forward on. And she would do it.

The village loomed ahead. Stone Carrier walked faster, Shadow slower. She clutched her spear, but her hands still shook. Demon's Mountain never felt as intimidating as the village did at this instant. Shadow's feet became boulders, barely inching forward.

Stone Carrier halted, waited till she was at his side.

Shadow drew up next to him, and suddenly that delicate line she had planned on walking snapped. She held her spear toward him.

His eyes widened.

"Please take this," she whispered.

Stone Carrier shook his head. "You have earned the right and honor to carry your spear. Carry it with pride."

"But the others—" Shadow fought back the stinging tears. "I—I cannot."

"You had the courage to face the demon."

Shadow pleaded. "This is different."

"You are correct. The villagers will not eat you." He rested his good hand on her shoulder. "Daughter, your courage and wisdom will not fail you now. Trust yourself as I trusted you on the mountain. As I trust you now." With the walking stick tucked under his arm, Stone Carrier limped on.

Taking a deep breath, Shadow scurried to catch him.

They walked side by side through the outer rows of homes. The surprised villagers joyously welcomed Stone Carrier home. Then they fell silent, staring at Shadow carrying a spear with her head held high.

Young boys ran ahead, proclaiming the news that Stone Carrier had finally returned.

The village plaza hummed and jostled. Men, young and old, pressed to congratulate Stone Carrier on his return. They fell back when they saw Stone Carrier with his walking stick and Shadow with her spear. A hush rippled the plaza.

Shadow coerced her shoulders to stay back and her spine straight. Her grass-like legs held her up somehow. Time lagged into eternity. She stared across the plaza to their home, aching to escape the villagers' stares and whispers. Yet she could not, would not, leave her father's side.

A face appeared at their door.

Shadow's heart stopped.

Mother stooped out the low door, a small, fur-covered bundle tucked in one arm. Her face gleamed with happiness as tears streamed down her face.

Stone Carrier said, "Go."

Shadow sprinted ahead.

Mother extended her free arm and encompassed Shadow.

Shadow's tears melded with her mother's as they hugged—Shadow's spear clutched in her left hand, and the fur bundle cradled in Mother's right arm.

A tiny sound meowed from within the fur bundle. A soft whimper, then a lusty cry added more tears to the home-coming.

Shadow peeked into the fur bundle. Still holding her spear, she reached for her new sister. She hesitated for an instant, looking at Mother.

Mother smiled and nodded her approval.

Her baby sister fit perfectly into the crook of Shadow's arm, as perfectly as her spear fit into her palm.

Insights from an Archaeologist

SHADOW'S VILLAGE, which we now call Elden Pueblo, lies on the outskirts of present-day Flagstaff, Arizona, near the slopes of the San Francisco Peaks. From around A.D. 1150–1275, it was a thriving village of two to three hundred people. Life there was fairly comfortable: The summer weather was kind to people and crops, and there was usually adequate water. Winters were harder, but houses were snug. Men, women, and children lived in a society in which each had clearly defined roles. Music and spirituality played an important role in village life, and careful adherence to ritual kept the society running smoothly.

Imagine living in a world without hardware or grocery stores, automobiles, plastic or metal containers, television, and all the other things *we* consider necessary. Every item needed for existence had to be made, either by the person who needed it or by a craft specialist. Every tool needed to make the item had to be made first. All food had to be grown, gathered in the wild, or hunted. Journeys were made on foot. Houses, clothing, bedding, dishes, tools, cooking utensils— all were made by hand from whatever was available: trees, yucca, stones, sand, clay, mud, animal hides and bones, or what could be traded for. No shiny metal axe to chop down a tree. No power saw to split wood. No pickup truck to move trade goods or building supplies from one area to another. If you needed something new, you invented it.

Yet, these people lived a full, rich life. They had close families. Storytelling was an important way to learn history and culture. Play and observation provided the rest of one's schooling. Everyone had many skills.

Women fetched water together, made baskets and clothing in each other's company, and ground corn side by side, so social interaction was constant. A close community was necessary for the survival of all.

Most people could make most of the necessities, but a few skilled specialists were making and trading their wares—usually objects too difficult to make without constant practice—for the other things they needed. Some pottery, stone tools, and baskets were simple enough for anyone to make. But some were clearly the products of people who did nothing else. In other words, a few people had something like a business.

When people settled into permanent communities instead of living a nomadic or seasonal life, crop growing (rather than mere gathering of wild plants) and the ability to store surplus food enabled more people to live together. Pottery flourished. (If you are moving every few days, do you want to be carrying heavy, breakable pots?) People came together to do projects, such as irrigation, for the good of the whole village. Political organization developed.

It was not an easy life, and the people living it had to be smart and very creative to survive. In years of adequate rainfall, life could be very good indeed. Drought years were more difficult, and a series of drought years *may* have been what eventually caused the villagers to leave their homes and move away.

—**Mary Swersey**
Professional Archaeologist